*Echoes By the Hearth Presents*

# *Ragnarök:*
# *The Twilight of the Gods*

*By*

## *Michael Wattam*

This book is a creative retelling of Norse mythology. While inspired by ancient sources, dialogue and narrative interpretation are the author's own.

ISBN:

eISBN:

Cover art: Runar.Hall

First Edition, 2025

Printed in the United Kingdom

# *Dedication*

*To everyone who ever felt the pull of ancient stories,*

*the weight of destiny, and the call to create.*

*May these pages honour the myths that shaped us.*

# *Acknowledgement*

This book was not written alone.

I owe so much to the people who encouraged me, challenged me, and reminded me why stories matter.

To the friends who listened, the family who supported me, and those who stood by me through every late night and uncertain moment—your belief carried me further than you know.

My gratitude also goes to the incredible community of storytellers, creators, and lovers of Norse myth who inspired this project from the very beginning.

Your enthusiasm, your discussions, and your shared passion for the old tales kept this fire burning.

Every message, every idea, every spark of excitement shaped this saga in ways I will never forget.

Thank you all for the support, the inspiration, and the faith that helped bring this book to life. May the old stories continue to guide us forward.

# *Table of Contents*

# Chapter 1
## Of Chains and Betrayal

In the fading age before the end, when twilight bled slowly into the bones of the world, the gods of Asgard turned wary eyes towards shadow.

Dreams soured.

Ravens whispered of ruin.

And from the ironwood, where roots drank deep of old blood, a wolf was born.

Fenrir, son of Loki and Angrboda, child of chaos and frost, emerged into the world already feared. He grew not by seasons, but by moments, towering with unnatural speed. His breath steamed with power. His eyes gleamed like molten gold. Yet though his shape was monstrous, he did not gnash or bite. Not at first.

But fear clung to him like a second pelt.

The gods had read the threads of fate. They knew what was woven: that one day, this wolf would swallow the All-Father whole.

They called him Doom-bringer. They called him Death-bound. They kept their distance, blades sheathed but fingers twitching.

All save one.

Tyr, god of justice and war, met the wolf not with steel, but with open hands. He fed him, trained him, and walked beside him. Tyr spoke not to a beast, but to a soul. And in Tyr's presence, the wolf grew quiet, his hunger tempered, his rage soothed.

Of all the gods, Fenrir trusted only him. But Odin's gaze reached farther than trust.

The All-Father had seen it: the final day, the snapping chain, the jaws opened wide.

Prophecy could not be unwound, only delayed.

And so, the gods whispered in secret halls. They did not speak of mercy. They spoke of binding.

Beneath the shadowed limbs of Yggdrasil, where roots drink from the bones of time, Odin stood alone.

The World Tree whispered secrets older than creation. Before him, Mímir's well rippled with prophecy. The All-Father gazed into its depths, and saw himself die.

A flash of gold.

A maw wide enough to swallow the sky.

Blood.

Then darkness.

Beside the waters, the severed head of Mímir stirred.

"You cannot unmake fate," the ancient voice rasped. "Only choose how you meet it."

Odin did not reply. He turned away, and gave the order.

The gods first forged Lædingr, thick as an oak trunk, heavy as mountain roots. Its black iron links groaned with runes. Four gods struggled to carry it.

With false smiles and honeyed words, they approached Fenrir, who towered now like a storm on legs. Still, he watched them with a hunter's calm.

"Is this the best the gods can do?" he said, teeth flashing. "I will wear it like a necklace."

They bound him. The last link clicked shut.

With a shrug and a roar, Fenrir shattered Lædingr. Shards of divine iron exploded across the plain. The gods paled.

Undeterred, they returned with Dromi, twice as thick, thrice as strong. Its core was carved with dark futhark, its links soaked in the dust of shattered oaths.

Even Thor had strained to lift it.

This time, Fenrir's resistance was swift and brutal. The earth split, and the sky shook as he broke free once more. The gods scattered like dry leaves.

"You test me like a beast," he growled. "But I am more than claws and rage."

Tyr said nothing.

Not yet.

At last, Odin turned to Svartalfheim, where the dwarves wrought the impossible.

They spun a ribbon thinner than breath, gleaming soft as silk, yet stronger than the laws of nature. They named it Gleipnir, and wove it from six things that could not be:

- The sound of a cat's footfall
- The beard of a woman
- The roots of a mountain
- The breath of a fish
- The spittle of a bird
- The sinews of a bear

When the gods returned with this thread of lies, Fenrir narrowed his golden eyes.

"That is no chain," he said. "It reeks of trickery."

Tyr stepped forward. "Then prove your strength. Show them there's no chain, no fate, that can bind you."

The wolf did not look away.

"I trust no word from them. But I trust you. Place your hand in my mouth, Tyr. Swear by your flesh this is no trick."

The wind stilled. Even the birds ceased to sing. Tyr hesitated.

He saw both paths: betrayal… or the end.

Not of the world, but of something sacred.

His voice cracked not with fear, but with guilt.

"You were not born to be a monster," he said softly. "But prophecy hunts us all."

He placed his hand between Fenrir's jaws.

"I swear it."

Fenrir lay still, and let them bind him.

When Gleipnir tightened, the world trembled.

Fenrir thrashed. The ground cracked. Stones split. But the ribbon held.

And then his eyes locked on Tyr. Betrayal blazed behind them.

"You lied," the wolf growled, low and ragged. "You lied to me."

In a single heartbeat, the jaws closed.

Tyr did not scream.

He turned his head away from the blood and looked, just once, towards Odin. The All-Father gave no answer. His face was carved from shadow.

Then came the snap of bone.

The gods drove a sword between Fenrir's jaws, wedging them open with steel. His roars fell to silence.

The gods cheered. But Tyr did not.

He turned, the stump of his arm weeping red, and walked away, leaving bloody prints across the stone. He refused Odin's praise. He spoke little in the days that followed.

He kept watch at the edge of Asgard, where the stars dipped low, waiting not for thanks, but for the doom he had helped delay.

Some say he returned to the wolf, long after others had forgotten.

"I never hated you," Tyr whispered. "I hated the choice."

Fenrir, bound and silent, gave no reply. But the gods knew this was not the end.

For with each setting sun, the wolf's hatred deepened.

His muscles coiled.

His purpose sharpened.

And prophecy waited like a buried blade.

*When fire walks and ice returns,*
*The wolf shall snap the woven lie.*
*Father shall fall, his blood on stone,*
*While justice limps beneath an empty sky.*

# Chapter 2
# *When Dreams Turn Dark*

In the golden halls of Asgard, where once laughter rang like bells and joy spilled from the very stones, a shadow began to stretch.

Baldur, beloved of gods and men, fairest in form and soul, had begun to dream.

Each night the visions came, dark and coiling, relentless as the tide. He saw himself lying lifeless on a battlefield glazed in frost, his skin pale as snow, his lips blue as twilight. Gods and mortals wept in silence. Ravens wheeled above a withered tree. Sacred fires flickered, guttered, died. A mother's scream rang out into a void that no longer knew stars.

He spoke little of it at first. But the dreams hollowed him.

The brightness that once lit Asgard like a second sun dimmed behind his eyes. His laughter faded. His step slowed. Even the air around him felt changed, quieter, watchful.

Frigg, Queen of Asgard, saw it.

She, who had soothed Odin's wounds beneath the gallows tree. She, who had sung lullabies through the storm of war. She, whose hands had steadied a world unravelling, now stood powerless before the terror creeping into her son.

This was not a matter of fate. Nor prophecy.

This was love.

The love that breaks laws. The love that bends gods to their knees. And so, Frigg rose.

Not as queen, but as mother.

She carried no sceptre. No crown. Her cloak flared behind her like a storm cloud, her hair unbound to the wind. She rode not in triumph, but in haste, and her voice, fierce and bright with fear, had already begun to shape the world.

To Muspelheim she rode first, land of flame and fury.

There, beneath Surtr's forges, where rivers of fire cracked and hissed like living serpents, she stood bare-faced before the blaze. The heat clawed at her skin, but she did not flinch.

"Swear you will not burn Baldur, son of Odin and Frigg."

The fire flared, hissed, then bowed low, its flame whispering:

"We swear."

To Niflheim she went next, realm of frost and sorrow.

She walked across black rivers that snapped like bone beneath her step. Spirits groaned from the ice. Cold crept into her marrow.

At Hvergelmir, the ancient well of venom and mist, she breathed into the frost:

"Swear you will not freeze him. Nor poison him."

The mist stirred. The well rippled. The ice gleamed like memory.

"We swear."

In Midgard, she wandered among forests and fields. She knelt beneath an old oak, gnarled and bent by storm and time. Her fingers pressed to bark scorched by lightning.

"Swear, tree, your limbs shall never harm him."

The tree creaked, shedding a single leaf into her palm.

"We swear."

She climbed wind-carved peaks and whispered to the skies. She stood before oceans and called out to Ægir, whose waves answered with a crashing roar.

She walked barefoot across salt plains and thorned fields. She met wolves in the deep woods, snakes in stony dens, and bears in ancient caves. She placed her hands on fur, on scale, on stone.

Each time, she asked:

"Swear you will not harm Baldur."

Each time, they answered:

"We swear."

In Svartalfheim, beneath the mountains, she descended into the choking smoke of the dwarves' halls.

She offered silver. She carved runes in the soot. The forge-masters, blackened by fire and craft, touched their hammers to their hearts.

"No blade of ours shall pierce him."

Even Jörmungandr, deep beneath the churning sea, turned in his coils and stirred at her plea.

"I will pass him by," the serpent hissed from the dark.

No stone would bruise. No beast would strike.

No fire, no storm, no sickness, no time.

Even death paused at her voice.

Frigg carved promises into the bones of the world.

She did not sleep. She did not eat. She wandered far, her hands blistered, her voice cracked, and in every whispering corner of the Nine Realms, she forced oaths from existence itself.

But west of Valhalla, in a grove so quiet even birds held their breath, a slender green shoot of mistletoe reached toward the sky.

There, Frigg did not go.

Too young, she thought. Too soft. Too small to matter.

When she returned to Asgard, her horse staggered with foam at its mouth. Her cloak was torn, her hands trembling.

The gods rushed to meet her, but she stood tall, exhausted, wild-eyed, radiant in grief and love.

"All things have sworn," she declared.

"My son shall not fall."

And there was rejoicing.

Odin smiled, though his brow creased. Thor raised his horn.

Freyja wept, joy laced with relief.

And Baldur, for the first time in weeks, laughed.

The sky brightened. The air sweetened. The halls filled with song. The light of Asgard blazed again.

And yet, far away, beyond memory's reach, in a grove of hush and shadow, the mistletoe swayed gently in the wind.

Unseen. Untouched.

And above it, a raven circled once…

…and flew on.

The fields of Gladsheim shimmered beneath a sky too bright to imagine sorrow.

Here, the gods had gathered, not in war or worry, but in joy. In celebration of Baldur, their shining one. The golden one. The god who seemed untouched by death, by pain, by time.

Laughter rang through the fields.

Golden grass rippled underfoot, soft as woven silk.

The branches above bore blossoms that never browned.

Mead flowed like music. Lyres sang to the rhythm of glad hearts.

They hurled axes and spears and stones at him, but every weapon glanced away like light on water. Fire coiled around his limbs and left no scorch. Even blades crafted by dwarves dulled upon his skin. The gods laughed like children who had never known grief.

Odin watched from Hliðskjálf, one hand curled around the arm of his high seat, the other resting on Gungnir. His one eye, hard and gleaming, did not blink.

Freyja wept with joy.

Thor bellowed with laughter, flinging boulders like pebbles.

And Baldur stood among them, unbowed, radiant. For a moment, he seemed eternal.

But on the edge of the gathering, a figure stood apart.

Höðr, blind, quiet, wrapped in the hush of shadow amidst all this blazing light. He turned his head toward the sound of joy, but his hands remained empty. He had no stone. No weapon. No place in the game.

Then another figure moved toward him. Smooth. Certain. Silent.

Loki, in his own skin once more, walked like smoke through sunlight. His face held no joy, no jest. In his hand he held a dart, no longer than a finger, pale and green.

Mistletoe.

Green as betrayal. Light as a whisper. Sharp as fate.

"Why do you not join them, brother?" Loki asked, voice soft as wind through grave grass.

"I cannot see," Höðr replied. "I have no weapon."

"Then let me lend you both." Loki smiled, thin, cold. "Let no brother be left out."

He placed the dart into Höðr's palm. It felt like nothing. Less than a breath. But the air grew heavy, thick with something unsaid. He guided Höðr's arm.

Curled his fingers around the shaft. Lifted it.

Released it.

"Just a jest," Loki whispered. And the dart flew.

It flew swift. It flew small.

It flew straight.

And it struck Baldur in the chest.

The gasp that followed seemed to silence the world.

He staggered, one step, then another, and fell to one knee. Laughter died.

Music stilled.

The sky dimmed, not with cloud, but as though the sun itself had blinked. Above, ravens circled in silence. Three now, not two.

Baldur's hand went to the wound, a tiny red flower blooming beneath his tunic.

"What... is this?" he whispered.

The gods surged toward him, but they moved too slowly, as though time itself had thickened. Frigg's scream was the first to break through.

She ran. She fell beside him, arms wrapping around him like roots around a dying tree.

"No," she breathed. "No, no... it's nothing. It's nothing."

"Mother," Baldur said, voice cracking like thawed ice. "I think... it's something."

She held him tightly. "I made the world promise. Fire, stone, beast, branch... they all swore. All but..."

"Mistletoe," he finished. His breath was shallow now. "The one you left out."

"Too soft… too small," she whispered. "You were meant to live forever."

"Nothing does," Baldur said. "Not even the stars. Maybe… maybe I was just the first."

Frigg sobbed, cradling him. "You are my vow. My morning. I sang your name before you were born."

"Then remember me in the dawn," Baldur said, eyes half-closed. "Let me rise with the sun, even if I'm gone."

Odin knelt beside them, his shadow stretching long.

His face was unreadable. But his eye, his one, burning eye, glimmered like a storm held back.

"You feared this," Baldur said.

"I did," Odin answered. "And still I let it come."

"Then don't waste it," Baldur whispered. "Find who did this. Stop what follows."

"By the gallows I once hung from," Odin vowed. "By the eye I gave. I will."

Baldur's voice faded to a whisper.

"I'm not afraid," he said. "Just… tired."

Frigg pressed her forehead to his.

"You are my light. I will carry you in every heartbeat. Every sunbeam."

He smiled, just barely.

And then, as a breeze stirred the grass around them, Baldur exhaled, and was still.

The moment shattered.

Frigg screamed, a sound no god should ever make. It tore across the Nine Realms like lightning through a tree. The sky cracked. Thunder rolled. Flowers withered. The air turned sharp with cold.

Where his blood touched the soil, the grass blackened.

And somewhere far below, deep in the roots of Yggdrasil, a thread snapped.

The gods knelt around him.

Freyja wept openly. Heimdall covered his face.

Thor stood frozen, his fists trembling.

No one spoke. No one dared.

Only one God moved.

Heimdall, ever-watchful, turned his gaze toward the edge of the field.

And there, just past the circle of grief, a figure walked away.

Tall. Cloaked. Unhurried. Loki.

Not running. Just... leaving.

There was no smile. No smirk. No boast in his step. Only distance. Only the quiet of someone who had already vanished inside himself.

Heimdall blinked. And Loki was gone.

No ripple in the grass. No footprint.

Only a single black feather drifting down from the sky.

And somewhere, in the deep places of the world, the future cracked open. Ragnarök had begun.

And the Nine Realms mourned.

Even the trees bent low. Even the mountains trembled. Even the rivers wept.

So beloved was Baldur that the death of one God felt like the breaking of all things.

But the story of sorrow was not yet finished.

The gods would try to unmake the death. They would beg, bargain, plead.

But death, once seated, is a guest who seldom leaves.

ᛏ

Grief lay heavy over the golden halls of Asgard.

Where once laughter soared like birdsong, now silence reigned, thick and unmoving, like fog on a battlefield. The high halls seemed dimmer, the walls robbed of their lustre. Gods walked like wraiths, shadows of themselves, their steps echoing through a kingdom that no longer knew joy.

Even the sun, once eager to crown Baldur's brow, hung low and pale in the sky, its warmth dulled to a muted haze. Wind sighed through the boughs of Yggdrasil like a mourner through a temple.

But even now, a thread of hope remained, thin, trembling, but unbroken.

From the silence stepped Hermóðr the Bold, son of Odin, brother to the fallen. His voice was steady, though his hands shook as he spoke:

"I will ride to Hel," he said. "I will plead for Baldur's return."

Odin, grim as the twilight hour, gave him the reins of Sleipnir, the eight-legged steed who had carried gods across worlds and into battle. The All-Father leaned close and whispered a single sentence into Hermóðr's ear, none but he heard it. Then he placed a hand on his son's shoulder, heavy as fate.

And Hermóðr rode.

Alone. Into the dark. Into the places beyond life and memory.

He rode for nine nights, and each night grew colder than the one before.

The stars thinned overhead. The sky twisted into shapes the mind could not hold. Shadows moved without light, and time staggered like a drunk man lost in dreams.

He crossed valleys where the mist wrapped tight around his throat like a noose. Spirits drifted at the edges of sight, faceless and pale, recoiling from Sleipnir's silver hooves.

Mountains rose like broken spears, jagged and cruel, their peaks clawing the heavens. Winds screamed down their flanks, carrying voices not of gods, nor mortals, nor the dead, something older. Something waiting.

Rivers of ink-black water cut through stone like forgotten veins. He crossed them in silence. They sang of endings.

Still, Hermóðr did not stop.

ᛏ

At last, he reached Gjallarbrú, the bridge that crosses the river Gjöll, where the dead pass silently into shadow.

The bridge gleamed with a spectral light, paved in golden stones that gave off no warmth, only memory. Beneath it, Gjöll whispered like a grave being dug too late. Every current carried a voice, every eddy a name.

At its centre stood a guardian: Móðgudr.

She was tall, cloaked in starlight and bones, her spear older than sun or stone. Her hair streamed behind her like smoke caught in moonlight. Her gaze pierced through to the soul.

As Sleipnir's hooves rang against the gold, the bridge groaned beneath their weight. Móðgudr raised her spear.

"Who are you," she asked, "that rides with the weight of love and sorrow so great it wakes the dead from their dreaming?"

Hermóðr dismounted. His breath misted in the cold.

"I am Hermóðr, son of Odin. I come to plead for the life of my brother, Baldur. I will not turn back."

Móðgudr's eyes narrowed.

"Many have come here, bearing love. Few return with what they seek. Will you pay the toll?"

"What toll?" he asked.

"Your fear. Your fate. Your future."

And the mist thickened.

Shadows stirred around him, not enemies, but possibilities. Visions twisted through the fog:

Baldur dying over and over. Odin weeping on a shattered throne. Sleipnir standing alone in a field of ash. Hermóðr himself, broken and forgotten, his journey a footnote in a saga no one would sing.

He clenched his fists.

"I will ride through death a thousand times if it means he lives again."

Móðgudr studied him long.

Then she lowered her spear.

"Then pass, son of Odin. But know this, Hel's bargains are not made with mercy."

Sleipnir crossed the golden bridge, and the mist swallowed all sound.

Beyond Gjallarbrú stood the walls of Helheim, high and silent, forged not from stone, but from stillness. Walls black as mourning cloth, etched with runes too ancient for even Odin's tongue. Cold radiated from them like breath from the grave.

Sleipnir leapt.

And they passed from the realm of the living into Hel.

The air changed. There was no colour. No scent.

No light, only a grey haze, like grief made manifest.

The mist clung to Hermóðr's skin, tasting of ash and old iron. Every footfall echoed in ways that defied the rules of space or time. The fog did not move. It breathed.

The Hall of the Dead rose before him, vast and still. Its pillars were carved from trees that had never known sunlight. Its roof groaned with the weight of forgotten names. Its floor was polished obsidian, but it reflected nothing.

Time did not move there. Even thought felt slow.

And at the centre of that frozen hush, seated upon a dais of dark ice, was Baldur. He was pale, but not broken.

A soft glow clung to his skin, not flame, not sunlight, but memory. He was not quite living, not truly dead. He was endurance. Dignity. A final echo that refused to fade.

Beside him sat Nanna, his wife, who had followed him in death. She held his hand in hers; fingers entwined like ivy on a grave. Her face bore the calm of someone who had shed all her tears and found something still beyond sorrow.

When their eyes met Hermóðr's, something passed between them, wordless, weightless. Like the first note of a song long unsung.

And they smiled.

But it was a smile tempered by resignation. Not grief, not anger, just a quiet knowing. They were glad to see him, but they did not rise.

They could not. Not yet.

While Hermóðr rode the storm-swept paths toward Helheim, another son of Odin wandered the golden halls of Asgard, unseen, unheard, drowning in silence.

Höðr, the blind god, sat alone in a long-abandoned courtyard, where the sun no longer reached and the wind carried only sorrow. Ivy crept along the stone walls like forgotten prayers, and the air tasted of ash and old rain.

His back pressed against a pillar carved long before his birth. In his lap, he held the broken shaft of the mistletoe dart, small, unremarkable, soaked in memory.

He turned it over in his hands, again and again, as if it might explain itself. As if its smoothness could confess the weight it had carried.

How could something so slight, so trivial, have felled the brightest soul in all the realms?

In the distance, he could hear them: gods pacing like mourners in a dream, their voices hushed, their footsteps hesitant. The sound of sorrow, of songs unsung. But none came to him.

No one spoke blame. No one offered comfort. No one looked at him.

And that silence cut deeper than any spear.

"Why did I throw it?" he whispered into the void. "Why did I listen?"

He remembered the voice, smooth as mead, warm as kin, guiding his hand. He remembered laughter. The reassurance. The lie.

And then the gasp. The thud of a body.

And the silence that never lifted.

"I would give my eyes," Höðr murmured, "to unsee what I never saw."

A wind stirred the courtyard. Cold. Sharp. Carrying with it the scent of storm and smoke.

Then, footsteps.

Measured. Heavy. Like grief made flesh.

Frigg appeared at the edge of the courtyard, her once-radiant face carved hollow with mourning. She did not wear her crown. Her cloak dragged the dust behind her. She was no longer the Queen of Asgard, only a mother broken beneath the weight of fate.

Höðr did not rise.

He bowed his head and held the dart tighter.

"Mother…"

She stood before him, unmoving. Her eyes fell to the fragment in his lap. Her hand lifted, almost reaching, but trembled. And stopped. She could not touch him. Not yet.

Not the son who had, however blindly, struck down her heart.

"I didn't know," Höðr said, his voice cracking like a frozen branch. "He told me it was a jest. That Baldur would laugh. That it was nothing."

Frigg sank to her knees before him, slowly, as though grief had hollowed her bones.

"It was not your will," she said, her voice more breath than sound, "but it was still your hand."

He turned his face away.

"I would have taken his place. I would beg Hel to take me instead."

Her eyes shimmered, but no tears fell. She had wept beyond weeping.

She reached to her side, unclasped a length of her tattered cloak, and laid it gently beside his hand. Faded blue, the colour she had worn when Baldur was born.

She did not speak again.

It was not forgiveness. But it was not rejection.

She stood and walked away; her footsteps lost in the wind.

And Höðr remained, alone with the shard of fate in his lap, his fingers tight around it, as if he could squeeze meaning from the wood.

He did not yet know that his death had already been chosen. That even now, the seed of vengeance stirred in Odin's heart,

A son not yet born, growing in silence, for the sole purpose of justice.

And the gods, once bound by love, now braced for war.

ᛏ

But fate does not forgive.

And vengeance walks faster than mourning.

That same night, as Baldur's pyre still smouldered and Frigg's screams echoed across the heavens, Odin left the halls of Asgard and walked alone beneath the branches of Yggdrasil.

The World Tree groaned in the windless dark. No stars shone through its canopy. No gods followed him.

The ravens circled above like storm-clouds. Even they kept their distance.

There, in the frozen silence, Odin sought Rindr, a jötunn of frost and stone, whose blood ran cold and old as glaciers. He did not come to her with gentleness, nor speak of love. This was not desire.

This was necessity.

This was the cruel bargain of prophecy.

From that union, in the deep hours before dawn, Váli was born. Not as a child.

But as a reckoning.

By sunrise, he stood full-grown, tall as his father, forged in silence. His limbs were hard as hammered steel, his gaze the cold gleam of a blade drawn without ceremony. No lullabies had touched him. No cradle had held him.

He bore no name but Purpose.

He asked no questions. Demanded no truth.

"You were made for one thing," Odin said. "Do not fail."

Váli said nothing. He did not need to.

ᛏ

Dusk fell over Asgard.

The once-golden sky had turned iron-grey, and the halls, though lit with flame, cast no warmth.

Still in the shadowed courtyard, Höðr sat motionless, his back against the ancient pillar. He had not moved since Frigg had left him. The broken shaft of mistletoe lay at his side, half-buried in fallen leaves.

He listened to the wind, waiting for something he could not name.

And then he heard it.

Not whispers. Not mourning. Footsteps.

Heavy. Measured. Inevitable.

He turned his face toward the sound.

He did not need to ask who approached.

"Have you come to kill me?" he said softly.

No answer.

"Then do it."

There was no struggle.

No shield raised. No blade drawn in defence.

Only the quiet fall of breath.

The soft rustle of a body sinking into stillness.

And the flutter of black wings above.

Váli, forged for this single moment, stood over him. He did not tremble. He did not gloat. His blade, slick with blood, caught no light. He simply turned, task completed, and walked into the deepening dark.

Höðr died not in battle, but in sorrow.

He slumped at the base of the pillar that had held his weight through long days of grief. His blind eyes stared skyward. One hand still clutched a corner of Frigg's torn cloak. The other brushed the edge of the mistletoe shaft.

The gods came too late.

From the high halls they ran, Thor, Freyja, even Odin himself. But none moved faster than Frigg.

She saw the shape crumpled in the courtyard. The blood. The broken son.

She knelt beside him, but he was already gone.

Her hand trembled against his brow. Her cloak, the one he still held, fluttered in her fingers like a memory trying to slip away.

And something inside her cracked.

"LOKI!"

She screamed it, not as a name, but as a curse. A roar of fury that shattered the sky.

"You've taken them both! My light and my shadow!"

Her voice rose, raw and wild, filled not just with grief, but with vengeance made sound. It echoed through the marble corridors, through the roots of Yggdrasil, down into the caverns where secrets sleep and monsters wait.

Above her, the ravens scattered. The wind fell still.

Even the flames bowed low.

And far away, across wild rivers and forgotten roads, wherever he had slipped,

Loki turned his head.

And smiled.

# Chapter 3
# *The Mist That Slew the Sun*

Hermóðr stepped forward and knelt before the throne of Hel, Queen of the Underworld.

She sat motionless at the far end of the hall. One half of her face was pale and cruelly beautiful, flesh unmarred, lips blue as ice. The other half was a death mask, skull bared to bone, teeth fixed in a grin no joy had ever touched. Her gaze held no warmth. Only gravity. Only the weight of endings.

She wore no crown. She did not need one.

Her throne was not carved but grown—twisted from root and sinew, knotted with grave-linen and strands of hair plucked from the heads of the dead. Behind her, a wall of ancient frost loomed like a frozen waterfall, and the mist that filled the air curled with the breath of a thousand forgotten souls.

Hermóðr's voice, though hoarse with grief, did not tremble.

"Please," he said. "Let Baldur return. All the Nine Realms mourn him. Without his light, the world dims. The seasons falter. Let it be undone."

For a moment, nothing moved. The gloom held its breath. Somewhere, far beyond the walls of that realm, a soul sighed and vanished.

Hel did not blink. Her eyes—one black as a drowned well, the other vacant as a grave—regarded him with the stillness of glaciers. She tilted her head slightly, as if hearing something distant, then finally spoke.

Her voice was low and grinding, like earth shifting beneath snow.

"If all things in the world, living and dead, will weep for Baldur, then he may go free."

She leaned forward. Her breath misted into the air, curling around her like smoke rising from cold ashes.

"But if even one creature refuses, if even one heart stays dry, then he shall remain. His light shall be mine."

It was no kindness.

No gift.

It was a test born of the dead—a cruel symmetry, a bargain as cold as her realm.

Something flickered behind her eyes—not pity, not hope. Perhaps inevitability.

Hermóðr bowed low. Behind him, Baldur stood silent, wrapped in his pale glow, his presence as sorrowful as a memory already fading. And in that realm where nothing moves quickly, even silence felt like a farewell.

The gods scattered across the Nine Realms, calling out to every creature, every current and mountain, every ember and star.

The world answered.

Trees wept sap like tears. Rivers turned grey with grief. Stones gleamed with moisture that had not come from rain. The sun dimmed. Birds stilled. Even wolves howled mournfully at the edge of the world.

It seemed that Baldur would return.

It seemed the light would rise again.

But in the far reaches of Jötunheim, beyond cliffs etched with runes too old to read, beneath storm-churned skies where crows flew in endless circles, a mountain rose without name. Its peak stabbed the heavens like a shattered crown. At its foot, half-hidden in moss and shadow, yawned a cave—a black wound in the world.

The mouth of the cave was choked with bramble and thorn, roots like twisted fingers clutching at stone. Brown water dripped from the ceiling, feeding a pool that reeked of rot. The air was thick and damp, rank with burnt hair, old blood, and something older still—betrayal steeped into rock.

Inside, a fire smouldered without warmth, casting green and sickly light across the walls. And beside it, Þökk sat.

Hunched beneath a ragged cloak of feathers and fur, she looked more corpse than crone. Her fingers were long and yellowed, her spine hunched, her face veiled in black so thin it fluttered when she breathed. If she breathed. When she moved, her bones crackled like branches underfoot.

The gods came to her: Freyja, her beauty wan beneath soot and sorrow; Heimdall, grim-eyed and unflinching; and Bragi, the silver-tongued skald, who carried no sword—only words.

They knelt.

"All things have wept for Baldur," said Bragi. "Stone and fire, root and wind. The stars mourn him. Only you remain."

Þökk said nothing at first. Then she laughed. It was a sound like dead teeth clacking together. No joy. Just bitterness. Just mockery.

"Baldur?" she rasped. "What has he ever done for me?"

Bragi stepped forward.

"He is the light of the Nine Realms. The promise of a better dawn."

Þökk spat into the fire.

"Let Hel keep what she has."

The flame hissed but gave no heat. Shadows flickered on the cave walls—longer than they should have been. Stranger.

Freyja's eyes narrowed. Something in Þökk's voice had changed. Too sharp. Too knowing. And then she saw it.

Near the fire, half-buried in the dust, lay a single black feather. Long. Perfect. Oiled and gleaming, untouched by ash. It did not match the faded plumage of Þökk's cloak. It gleamed like memory.

Heimdall inhaled sharply. His gaze swept the cave, measuring every shadow.

Freyja opened her mouth—to speak, to accuse—but something stopped her.

The gods said nothing more. They turned and left the cave, their hearts heavier than when they had entered. Behind them, the fire sputtered low. One shadow lingered longer than the rest. It bent. It grinned.

Some say Þökk was just a crone—bitter and forgotten.

But others whispered, as they left the mountain:

"That was no giantess."

"That was Loki."

And so, Baldur, beloved of all, remained in the land of the dead.

Waiting.

Dreaming.

Until the end of all things.

The gods turned their faces from the light.

And far below, in the shadows of grief, the first roots of Ragnarök began to grow.

# Chapter 4
# Shackles Forged in Silence

The skies wept ash the day they hunted the Trickster.

Loki Laufeyjarson, flame-born, silver-tongued, fled across the Nine Realms with blood on his hands and a serpent's grin carved into his lips. Baldur was dead—shining Baldur, beloved of all—and the world dimmed for it. The sun withdrew behind shrouds of mourning. Winds carried only whispers of blame and thunder.

Still, Loki ran.

He danced along the broken branches of Yggdrasil, slipped between folds of storm and shadow, laughter rising like smoke through cracks in the world. It was laughter warped by grief, jagged with guilt, echoing like a shattered mirror.

But the gods would not be denied.

Thor led the hunt, red-bearded and roaring, Mjölnir clenched like judgement in his fist.

Týr rode beside him, justice in his one hand, the other a memory.

Freyja, cloaked in falcon feathers, eyes like whetted blades.

Heimdall, the watcher, saw the Trickster's path through mist and lie, and led them to Midgard—

—to a place where cliffs split like skulls and a river thundered through stone.

There, beneath the crashing water, a salmon flashed silver.

Loki.

He slid beneath the torrent, hiding in root and rock, winding like a thought too swift to seize. But the gods knew his guises.

They cast a net—not of rope, but of unbreakable thread, spun from starlight and rune.

Thor waded into the gorge, his arm like the will of the storm itself. With a single thrust, he caught the salmon by the tail.

The fish twisted, shrieking in motion—but Thor held.

Dragged from the river, Loki writhed and changed, coughing up water, his limbs resuming shape. His face, slick with foam and fury, turned defiant.

"So, this is your justice?" he spat. "A net for a voice, a hammer for a truth."

"You are no truth," Thor growled. "You are rot with a tongue."

Freyja stepped forward, her voice like flint:

"You betrayed us. You betrayed me."

Loki bared his teeth.

"You betray yourselves. You sit on your thrones, pretending peace. But peace was a lie made from Baldur's smile. I only showed you the cracks."

And then came Odin.

Shadow-draped. One eye like a storm held at bay. His ravens circled overhead, silent.

He stepped close, not as a king, but as a brother once betrayed.

"Why did you kill Baldur?"

The question fell like the end of an age.

Loki's smile faltered.

He looked away, then back. His voice, when it came, was low.

"Because you loved him more."

A pause. The mask slipped.

"You gave me a seat, Odin. But never your heart. I was your shadow. Your convenient chaos. But Baldur… he was your light."

Odin said nothing.

"He was too perfect," Loki hissed. "He made us all lesser. I didn't kill him—I freed him. I ended the illusion."

Odin's voice was thunder stilled.

"You lit the fire."

Loki's smile returned, twisted and sharp.

"Then let me burn with it."

ᛏ

They dragged him beneath the world, past root and rock, to a cavern older than war, older than gods.

Stone walls wept. Stalactites hung like frozen fangs. The air smelt of damp blood and long-held rage. The heart of the world beat slowly here, as if listening.

The gods formed a circle. Loki lay at its centre, bleeding, silent.

A single torch burned, casting shadows like scars.

Týr spoke first.

"End him. For justice."

Frigg, voice hollow, whispered:

"What justice? My son is gone. Both my sons."

Skadi stepped forward, her presence sharp as ice.

"Let him suffer. Let his screams feed the winds."

Freyja said, "No clean death. Let him drown in what he gave us."

Thor raised his fist.

"Bind him. Cast him into the Void."

But Odin raised a hand.

"Not the Void. Let the world hear what he's become."

He turned to Sigyn, who stood at the edge, her face pale, her hands clenched.

"Do you still call him husband?"

She nodded once.

"Even now?"

Again, a nod.

Then Odin gave his sentence:

"He shall be bound beneath the world, in sight of no one but the stones. And they will echo with his screams until the end of days."

Chains could not hold what Loki had become. Not iron. Not rune. Not spell.

So, Skadi spoke the unthinkable:

"Then bind him with his own blood."

They brought forth his sons—Vali and Narfi, born of Sigyn.

A curse carved in runes was spoken. Vali screamed as he was twisted into a wolf—mind shattered, heart gone.

Sigyn cried out.

But Vali lunged.

And Narfi died.

Ripped. Torn. Left in a ruin of flesh and steam.

The gods, silent and grim, took Narfi's entrails—wet with death— and twisted them with seiðr into bonds that no world could break.

Loki was stretched across a jagged slab. His arms wrenched wide. His legs pinned. His spine arched. His chest pressed against unyielding stone.

Above, they hung a serpent—its belly split so that venom dripped, slow and steady, drop by drop, onto his face.

Each burn was an agony forged in the marrow of myth.

And Loki screamed.

It was not rage.

Not regret.

It was a scream older than words. A sound that bent roots, split sky, and sent wolves howling in their dens.

The mountains trembled. Seas surged. Even Yggdrasil shivered.

And through it all—Sigyn stayed.

Only one remained.

Sigyn, barefoot and grief-worn, descended into the bowels of the world. The silence there was not absence, but weight—a silence that pressed on the bones and thickened the breath. Her gown was torn, soaked in ash and salt. Her hands were raw. Her hair clung to her face like the ghosts of forgotten dreams.

In her arms she bore a simple bowl.

Unadorned. Unshaped by pride.

A thing of no name—yet it became the last act of love in the Nine Realms.

She knelt beside her husband.

Above him, the great serpent hissed, suspended from the roots of the earth. Its black belly swayed ever so slightly, and from its fangs the venom fell—slow, steady, endless.

Loki lay bound on the cold slab, arms outstretched, spine twisted against the rock, the magic-forged entrails of his son biting deep into his flesh. His skin was blistered. His lips were cracked. His voice, when it came, was a rasp between tremors.

"Sigyn…"

She did not look up.

"You shouldn't have stayed," he whispered. "You should have gone with the others."

Still, she held the bowl.

"They took our sons," Loki said, voice fraying. "Twisted Vali. Tore Narfi. Made their deaths into a cage… and still I burn."

Nothing.

"I didn't want this," he breathed. "Baldur… it was never meant to end like this."

The bowl trembled faintly in her grip, catching each drop before it touched his face.

"Please," Loki whispered, desperation now bleeding through his defiance. "Speak to me. Hate me if you must. Just say something."

But Sigyn only caught the venom.

When the bowl brimmed, she rose carefully, hands steady, arms aching, and stepped to the side to pour its poison away into a crevice worn deep into the stone.

In that breathless pause, a single drop slipped through.

It struck his cheek like molten fire.

Loki screamed—a sound that tore through the cavern like a storm through hollow mountains. He writhed, chains groaning, the stone beneath him cracking with the strain of his anguish.

But then she returned.

She knelt again. She raised the bowl. She said nothing.

Not out of coldness. Not in cruelty.

But in love.

Love that bore no illusions.

Love that did not forgive—but would not abandon.

Her silence was heavier than the serpent, deeper than Helheim, and more crushing than Mjölnir's blow. It was the silence of a vow made long ago, when they first joined hands beneath a younger sky.

And so, it went.

Drop by drop.

Scream by scream.

Century after century.

The gods had chained him—but not her.

And somewhere far above that buried cave, in the realm of Midgard,

the snow began to fall.

The wind bit sharper.

The harvests waned.

Men huddled closer to their fires, whispering tales of wolves and endings.

The world did not break in thunder.

It began, softly—

With silence.

With snow.

With the slow, unbearable patience of fate.

Ragnarök had begun.

# Chapter 5
# The Frost Before the Flame

They did not hear the scream beneath the world.

They did not see the venom fall, or the woman kneeling to catch it.

But Midgard felt it.

Something shifted in the marrow of the world. The soil grew still. The birds flew south and never returned. The skies hung heavy with a silence that would not lift.

Snow came too early.

At first, the people welcomed it — a crisp frost on the thatch, a reason to huddle closer around the hearth, to tell old tales and drink deep. But spring never followed. No thaw came. The ice remained. The rains did not fall.

The rivers shrank to pale threads weaving through cracked banks. The ground turned to stone beneath the farmers' hands. Crops curled in on themselves, seeds never waking. Cows calved stillborn. The goats refused to bleat.

In a village clinging to the edge of the mountains, frostbitten and thin, an old woman rose beside a dying fire.

"This is no season of men," she rasped. "This is the breath of the end. Mark it."

Some laughed — young, brave, desperate.

"The gods will not forsake us," one said, his blade catching firelight as he sharpened it with trembling hands.

"They already have," murmured another, not looking up.

Children fell ill — first coughing, then fever, then silence. Mothers lit candles and whispered prayers to gods who no longer answered. The altars grew cold.

One morning, a hunter followed deer tracks into the deep wood. At the edge of a frozen stream, he found not prey, but a great grey wolf, waiting in silence.

It did not growl.

It did not run.

It only watched.

Measured.

And turned away.

The hunter never returned.

The second winter came — and did not leave.

There was no planting. No thaw. No hope. Only cold layered upon cold, a weight pressing against the bones of the world. The wind no longer whistled. It screamed, like beasts mourning their dead.

The skies turned grey and stayed grey. The sun became a rumour, a pale smear behind unmoving clouds. The stars, when they appeared, were not the same — faint, flickering, foreign.

Villages curled inward, drawing their walls close. Fires were hoarded like gold. Salted meat became sacred. A heel of bread could fetch a knife.

In one frost-shrouded town, two brothers stood over the frozen body of their father. One held a loaf. The other, an axe.

"You've already eaten today," snarled the elder.

"So did he," the younger hissed, nodding to their father. "Look where it got him."

They lunged.

Steel rang. Blood steamed in the snow.

In the wilds, warbands formed from what had once been men — faces daubed in ash, breath clouding like smoke, blades nicked and red from constant use. They no longer sang. They no longer prayed.

Some cursed Odin's name with cracked lips. Others forgot the gods entirely.

Temples stood hollow, their altars buried in ice. The runes carved on stones grew soft and unreadable beneath the snow.

Fathers barred their sons from the hearth.

"There is no more 'ours,'" one said to his daughter, clutching the last of their salted meat with shaking hands. "Only what I can hold."

At night, the howling came — long, low, not quite wolf.

Women clutched their children tighter, whispering stories of warmth, of light, of gods that once answered.

The children did not believe them.

Overhead, the ravens gathered, silent as judgement, black shapes watching from snow-laden rooftops.

By the third winter, names no longer mattered.

Words froze on the tongue. Maps were useless. Memories became dangerous luxuries.

The wind had teeth — jagged, tearing — and it howled through the bones of long-dead forests. Snow fell not in flurries but in thick, blinding veils, smothering the world in white silence. Entire villages vanished beneath the drifts, their rooftops buried, their doors sealed shut forever. Roads became rumours. Rivers became tombs. Trees split and fell under the sheer weight of ice, like giants bowing to some unseen doom.

There was no more trade. No messengers. No songs.

No sun.

Children were born having never seen it — only the dim grey sky that never changed. Mothers taught them to walk by starlight... and to run when they heard the footsteps of men.

In a half-buried hall near a frozen fjord, survivors huddled around a dead fire, breathing in silence. Among them, an old skald with fingers black from frost whispered to the shadows:

"Three winters. No spring. This is the end the seers saw. The Fimbulvetr."

A voice from the dark: "What comes after?"

He did not blink. "The wolves," he said. "And then the fire."

By then, men had become monsters.

They no longer came with words, but with torches and blades. They took what they hungered for and burned what they could not carry. They wore no clan marks. They answered to no chieftain, no god, no law. Only hunger. Only rage.

Once, a man killed his own brother for a crust of bread — and did not weep after.

"Brother against brother," the old woman had warned.

And now it was not prophecy.

It was memory.

One night, a girl wandering beneath the breaking stars saw a black feather drift down from the sky. It did not fall like a snowflake. It did not belong to any bird. But she knew — deep in the marrow of her bones — that something had begun.

No prayers reached Asgard. No visions came from Mímir's well. No dreams stirred the bones of the Völva.

Midgard did not fall in fire or thunder.

It froze, alone, unwept.

And the people endured the silence until even hope forgot its name.

And yet...

Deep beneath root and rock, beneath the frost-hardened bones of the earth, where no birds sing and no sun has ever touched, Loki still writhed in his bonds.

The chains — forged from the entrails of his son, Narfi — bit deep. They were not only bindings of flesh, but of fate. Each link sang with pain and betrayal. Each held fast not just his body, but the storm within him.

Above him, the serpent hung like a curse made flesh. Its coils shifted in silence, eternal and cruel. Venom dripped with maddening rhythm, slow as time, precise as hate — burning like falling stars across Loki's face.

And beside him knelt Sigyn.

She, who had not fled.

She, who had lost more than most.

She, who still endured.

Her hands, once gentle, now trembled. The plain wooden bowl she bore felt heavier with each day, though it held only drops. But grief makes even light burdens unbearable. Her eyes, rimmed with red, stared not at Loki — but at the venom.

Still, she held it.

Still, she caught every burning tear from the serpent's maw.

And when she rose — when she turned to empty the bowl — the venom struck.

It struck Loki's face, his chest, his soul.

And Loki screamed.

Not a scream of pain alone, but of memory, of rage, of the world twisting into something it was never meant to be.

The cavern shook.

Stone cracked like bone.

Yggdrasil shivered in its roots.

The seas surged. Mountains moaned.

Children in distant huts awoke with tears on their faces, not knowing why.

And in his torment, Loki began to dream.

Dreams soaked in venom, scorched by memory, shaped by a hate older than war.

He saw Fenrir, golden-eyed and vast, loping across a sky torn in two, the sun bleeding in his wake.

He saw Jörmungandr, the World Serpent, rise from the blackened deep — his coils splitting islands, his breath poisoning clouds.

He saw Hel, still and unmoving, her throne of bone cradling her silence. Her eyes said nothing. But they promised everything.

He saw the roots of Yggdrasil split with flame and frost.

He saw gods screaming.

He saw the world ending.

And he saw himself.

No longer bound.

Standing tall at the helm of Naglfar — the ship of the dead — its sails stitched with silence, its hull groaning with the weight of forgotten names.

His eyes burned like twin coals. His voice rode the wind like prophecy.

And in the dark, Loki whispered through scorched lips:

*"The world will burn for what was done to me.*

*The gods will drown in the lies they fed me.*

*And I will be there —*

*not to lead...*

*but to laugh."*

Above him, Sigyn returned.

She sat, arms trembling, bowl cradled in weary hands.

She did not look at him.

She did not speak.

But she wept.

Not for herself.

Not even for the man she once called husband.

She wept for the fire she saw in his eyes.

For the silence that would come after his scream.

For the world —

and all that would not survive it.

ᚠ

In the frozen dark beneath the world-tree, where time once flowed like song, the Norns sat in silence.

Urd, Verdandi, and Skuld — the weavers of fate, the daughters of night — gathered at the Well of Urðr, their hands still, their thread unspun.

42

The well, once bright with shimmering visions, now lay sheathed in ice. Its surface no longer danced with the ripples of becoming, but lay flat and lifeless, like the eye of a corpse. Where once futures bloomed like petals across the water, now only shadows gathered — thick, unmoving, mute.

The loom beside them stood idle. The spindles sagged. The threads were frozen in place, caught mid-weave, mid-thought, as though time itself had drawn breath and refused to exhale.

Frost clung to the edges of their cloaks like sorrow made visible. Around them, the roots of Yggdrasil creaked with strain, great cracks spreading like veins through bark older than gods. Sap leaked like blood into the frozen earth.

The eldest, Urd, leaned over the well. Her pale eyes, once deep as the world's memory, stared into the clouded depths. She did not blink.

*"We can no longer see the end,"* she whispered. Her voice, hoarse with centuries, drifted like smoke. *"Only that it comes."*

Verdandi bowed her head, her hands folded in her lap like wilted petals. Her mouth moved, but no sound followed.

Skuld — who speaks only of what is yet to be — said nothing at all.

For the first time since the first dawn… fate itself was silent.

And overhead, the roots of the world groaned, trembling toward a fall.

ᚨ

From the east, the wolves stir —

shadows with golden eyes and hungers that no name can hold.

Their breath steams in the dark, and the scent of blood is already in their mouths.

From the south, fire flickers beneath the waves,

and deep in the ocean's black belly, the World Serpent coils and turns.

The sea groans as his venom seeps through the water like ink.

From the north, Naglfar creaks against its mooring —

a ship born of unburnt nails, its hull stitched with silence and rot.

Each death in the Nine Realms feeds it, and the tide inches higher.

From the west, Heimdall stands alone upon the broken span of Bifröst.

His fingers clutch Gjallarhorn, knuckles white with waiting.

His gaze never wavers from the horizon that dares not break.

And still — it snows.

The wind does not move.

The gods do not speak.

The stars do not blink.

# Chapter 6
# The Howl, The Helm, The Harbinger

For an age unmarked by sun or season, the wolf lay still.

Far beneath the roots of Yggdrasil, in a hollow carved by fear and prophecy, Fenrir slept — not in peace, but in punishment. Stone pressed down upon him like a second sky. Runes burned cold across his limbs. Silence clung like frost to every breath.

The gods had sealed him here long ago — buried beneath their dread, their guilt, their unspoken truth. He had not howled since. Not since Tyr's blood ran down his throat. Not since the sword was driven between his jaws.

And so, he waited.

The years turned. The Nine Realms changed. But Fenrir did not move. No starlight found him. No birdsong reached him. Only stillness. Only darkness. Only the memory of a world that had cast him away.

But time wears all things thin.

Now, above, the snow no longer melts. The sun staggers in its arc. Men forget the names of gods. The fabric frays.

And in the depths, the silence broke.

A twitch of muscle.

A crack in the stone.

A growl, low and thunderous, coiling through the earth like a buried drumbeat.

Gleipnir held — forged from six impossibilities — but it groaned, fibres stretched past fate's own limits. It sang like a thread drawn to its final note. The wolf opened one golden eye.

And though the world above did not yet know it... the end had opened its jaws.

Tyr, God of law, honour, and sacrifice, stood alone at the edge of the world.

The plain before him was stripped of colour, a stretch of lifeless frost and cracked stone. No birds flew. No banners stirred. Only silence and wind — a wind that sang of endings.

He had not looked upon the wolf since the day of betrayal. Since Gleipnir was pulled tight. Since his hand was lost between the jaws of prophecy. He remembered that moment not as pain, but as a fracture — in trust, in order, in the gods themselves.

Now he stood sentinel once more, his sword resting against his knee, not raised. His shield hung slack on his back, not lifted. The stump of his right wrist was bound in old leather, the scar tissue pale as frostbite — a vow he had paid in blood, a price no one else would offer.

The wind howled like a dirge across the wide and hollow land. Tyr stared into it, unmoving. His voice, when it came, was low — not to be heard, but to be remembered.

"I bound you for peace," he said. "But peace is only ever a pause in war. I gave them justice... but they answered with silence."

No one replied. The wind tore at the rocks and moved on.

But Tyr felt it. Beneath his feet, deeper than root or rune, something shifted — a faint vibration in the bones of the world. Not a quake. Not yet.

A breath.

The wolf stirred.

And Tyr, jaw tight, placed his one hand upon his sword. The reckoning he had tried to delay now came with the weight of all unspoken truths. And still, he did not flinch. For if this was the end... he would meet it standing.

ᚠ

The wolf dreamed in darkness. But his dreams had soured.

Beneath the roots of Yggdrasil, where light could not reach and time moved like tar, Fenrir stirred. His muscles rippled — slow, immense — like rivers cracking under winter's final weight. Breath steamed from his nostrils. Claws scraped against stone, sending tremors through the buried bones of the earth.

He felt it. A loosening. A shift. The first fray in the leash the gods had sworn could never fail.

Gleipnir was breaking.

Not by brute force — not yet — but by the erosion of what once held the worlds together. The gods had turned their gaze toward mortal squabbles. Mortals had turned their blades on one another. Order rotted in silence.

And so, the wolf woke.

He rose — vast, terrible, ancient — and the ribbon sang a final, shrieking note. It tore. Not like cloth, but like fate unspooling.

Fenrir broke free.

The ground convulsed. Stone shattered like eggshells. Mountains split down their spines, jagged wounds beneath a sky already beginning to bleed.

In Asgard, Heimdall froze. His hand flew to Gjallarhorn. His breath caught. The final hour had come.

In Jötunheim, the frost giants stirred. Ancient kings of ice raised their heads from glacial thrones. Eyes like frozen stars opened for the first time in ages.

In Niflheim, Hel leaned forward on her throne of bone, still as death. She said nothing. But her gaze, fixed on the horizon, did not blink.

And deep beneath the world, where venom kissed stone, Loki smiled. His eyes caught fire. His voice slithered into the dark like a blade:

"The wolf is loose. The sky will bleed. The spear shall break. The last game begins."

Then came his laughter — cracked and wild, broken and beautiful — the laughter of a god who had waited far too long for the world to end.

ᛏ

In Niflheim, beneath the roots of all things — where warmth had never reached, and even memory froze solid — Hel stirred.

Her hall, Éljúðnir, groaned like a dying god. Frost-slick walls split with the sound of bone breaking, and stone pillars wept with melting rime as the wind of the dead stirred once more. The great gate, rimed in soul-ice and sealed for an age, exhaled its first breath in silence.

Above her throne, the banner of the Underworld — black as sorrow, tattered by time — fluttered for the first time in countless winters. As if the realm itself had drawn breath again.

And Hel rose.

Half her face was smooth, pale, serene — beauty untouched by time or breath. The other half: skull and sinew, a ruin of bone and rot. Her gaze, split between life and death, passed over her cold dominion. Where others saw decay, she saw judgement. Where others saw monsters, she saw witnesses.

She had waited long.

She had watched the Nine Realms rot. She had watched men burn offerings to Odin and Thor, carving prayers into gold while their own dead were left unburied in ditches, or forgotten in shallow graves. She had seen names fade from runestones. Ancestors silenced. The quiet dead exiled from song and memory alike.

She had heard the long scream of her father echo through stone and venom. And still she waited. Silent. Patient. Absolute.

Now, the silence cracked.

"The chains are broken," she whispered, her voice soft as snowfall — yet it rang through the frost like a bell tolling at the end of time. "The gods will answer for what they buried."

And with arms outstretched, Hel summoned her army.

They did not come with trumpets. They did not march with banners. They rose — forgotten.

Children lost in snowdrifts, frozen with no names spoken over them. Mothers who bled on cold stone, their lullabies never heard. Warriors felled in shame or silence, denied Valhalla. Kings entombed without song. Bastards. Betrayers. Lovers who died alone. Wanderers who perished in places no skald would ever walk.

Eyes snapped open beneath the ice. Fingers reached through frostbitten soil. Shapes formed in the gloom.

And Hel spoke — not in wrath, but in remembrance:

"You were cast out. But I see you. I name you. I raise you now."

Across Niflheim, the dead obeyed. They did not cry out. They did not wail.

They stood.

And beneath them, something stirred.

In the depths of the black sea between worlds, Naglfar strained at its mooring. No mortal vessel could bear such a burden. It was not carved by hand nor blessed by the gods. It had grown — a slow birth of horror — shaped from the untrimmed nails of the unburied dead.

Fingernails. Toenails. Bone slivers and rot. The cast-offs of those left unnamed, unmourned, unburnt.

It swelled on waves thick as oil, pushed by tides made of grief and silence. The ice that bound it cracked with the sound of centuries breaking.

A ship of silence. A ship of shame.

Each nail a soul unfreed. Each plank a broken promise. Every seam wept the cries of those denied passage. Every rib hummed with grief too long buried.

It did not creak like wood. It whispered. Soft and low — like wind through a graveyard, or breath behind a locked door.

It had waited through centuries, anchored in ice thicker than time, rocking on seas black as regret. It drank the stillness of Midgard, the apathy of men, the forgetfulness of gods, and it grew fat on the neglect of both.

And now, its black hull shuddered like a beast long starved. Its sail, stitched from sinew and skin, unfurled with a shriek that echoed across the void. No wind touched it, yet it billowed — filled by the breath of the forsaken.

Chains snapped. The mooring ice cracked and exploded outward, splinters of frost scattering like shattered bones. The sea beneath frothed — not with salt, but with blood. And from that red tide, Naglfar surged forward: no oars, no captain... only purpose.

It carved a path toward the mortal shore, prow cutting through mist like a blade through memory. And aboard it... the dead.

Not silent now. They stood shoulder to shoulder, eyes hollow, armour rusted, their voices rising in a low and ancient chant. A dirge not of sorrow, but of return. And at the side of the helm, waiting still, stood Hel. Leaving a space for someone to take command.

And soon… Loki would come to claim it.

ᚠ

The earth groaned with the weight of ancient pain.

Far beneath Midgard's frostbitten crust, in a cavern carved from sorrow, silence, and the bones of forgotten ages, the last chain began to fray. It did not snap with sudden fury. It unravelled — undone by time, by vengeance, and by the slow decay of the order that once dared bind gods.

The iron-blooded runes, etched deep into stone and oath, had dimmed. Their power, once sharp as judgement, had dulled into rust and regret.

And then — with the tremble of fate, and the scream of gathering storm — Loki stirred.

His limbs, long stiff with punishment, stretched for the first time in many moons. The slab beneath him cracked like bone under a god's heel. Above, the serpent writhed in sudden panic — its venom still dripping, still burning — and at his side, Sigyn, ever faithful, faltered. Her arms shook. Her face was hollow with grief unspoken.

And then — the bowl slipped.

Venom fell like molten ruin. And Loki screamed.

It was not a cry. It was calamity. A sound like a dying star. A scream that broke the roots of the world. Mountains buckled. Valleys split wide. Birds fell from the skies, their hearts stopped mid-flight.

The walls shuddered. The bindings fell like lies undone. The serpent hissed and vanished into the black.

Scarred.

Seared.

Laughing through blood and fire.

Loki rose.

Not a trickster now. Not a prisoner. But a reckoning, walking on two feet.

He came to Naglfar on winds that reeked of ash and ruin. His cloak hung in scorched tatters, his hair a snarl of smoke and storm. The sea split before him, black and boiling, and the dead — those denied by gods and forgotten by kin — parted in silence at his step.

He boarded the ship of nails not as an intruder, but as a king returned to a throne of bone. As though this ending had waited for him alone.

At the helm stood Hel. Her gaze met his — eyes dark as drowned stars, half her face smooth and silent as a tombstone, the other stripped to the skull, a beauty sculpted by death. She did not smile.

"Do you remember me?" she asked, voice thin as frost on glass.

Loki stepped close, brushing a coal-black lock from the bone-white cheek.

"Always," he said. "We were all cast out. But now we rise."

No oath was needed. No embrace exchanged. They stood together — father and daughter. God and Queen. Flame and frost.

Bound not only by blood, but by betrayal. By silence. By the grave injustice that made them monsters in the eyes of gods.

Naglfar groaned beneath their feet — its hull stitched from nail and neglect, weeping with the weight of centuries. Its sail of skin caught the wind, swollen with doom. And the ship began to move.

Toward the shore.

Toward the storm.

Toward the end of all things.

# Chapter 7
# *Watchful Eyes and Withering Hearts*

High in Asgard, where golden halls once rang with laughter, Frigg stood alone before Baldur's empty chamber.

The air held no warmth. No birdsong. No wind. Only silence — a silence that pressed against the walls like grief made flesh.

Dust lay like ash upon the stone. The bowl that once cradled her son's light now brimmed with shadow, its surface dull and lifeless.

She reached out with trembling fingers, tracing the old runes etched deep into the wall, wards of protection, the names of stars, lullabies hummed through long-forgotten winters. They were cold now. Cold as the grave. The magic in them had faded.

Her touch came away stained with dust, the colour of bone. Her breath misted the window. Beyond the glass, the clouds gathered low and grey, curling like smoke from a slow-burning world.

She had seen all of this — the loss, the war, the fall of gods. The visions had never left her. And yet, knowing had changed nothing.

"What use is foresight," she whispered, her voice thin and cracking like hoarfrost underfoot, "when none will listen? Even Odin, for all his wisdom, walks into the end with his eye open."

A raven landed on the ledge, feathers slick with rain, its gaze black as prophecy. It cocked its head. Said nothing.

Frigg did not flinch. She only stared, as if daring it to bring worse news than what her heart already carried.

In the far distance, thunder rolled. And from the edge of the world, the sea began to rise.

ᛏ

In Vanaheim, where summer once ruled like a golden king, all things began to die.

The orchards had dropped their fruit too soon. The vines had curled into withered claws. The barley fields — once his pride, once his joy — stood yellowed and broken, their stalks bent not with grain, but with grief.

The sky sagged under a ceiling of grey. The air tasted of dust and drought. The rivers, once wide with meltwater, ran shallow over cracked stone.

Freyr stood alone among the ruins of his garden.

No songs. No harvest. No sword. He had given that away — his shining blade, the one forged to stand against Surtr's flame. Not in battle. Not in duty. But for love.

For Gerðr, the frost-veined giantess who once looked at him with glacier eyes and thawed beneath his longing. He had bargained with fate itself to win her hand. And fate, smiling, had taken more than he could afford to lose.

"I gave away what I would now die to keep," he murmured. The words fell softly, like dry petals in the wind. "But I will not curse love. Not even now."

In his hands, he held only a pair of antlers — once on the brow of a great stag, polished by time and prayer. A token of the wild. A relic of harvest. They were heavy with memory, yet fragile in the face of war.

Still, he moved. He stepped through the patterns of battle, the sacred dance of earth and steel. Each motion slow, precise. Each sweep of the antlers a memory of what once was. Each turn a farewell — to orchards, to summers, to joy.

He struck the air as though threshing the last sheaves of wheat. He moved not like a warrior, but like a farmer casting seed into ash.

And he knew. He knew the antlers would shatter. He knew he would fall when Surtr came with his sword of flame. But he did not lower his gaze.

He stood his ground — last god of green things, of plenty, of peace, in a world that no longer bloomed.

†

At the edge of the sky, where the Rainbow Bridge arched from breath to flame, Heimdall stood alone.

Bifröst shimmered beneath his feet — but its colours ran thin, bleeding at the edges like oil on water. The hues no longer sang. They strained, quivered — like a harp string drawn too tight.

Heimdall paced its length in silence, every step an oath. His eyes, bright as newborn stars, saw the tremble of all things: the groaning roots of Yggdrasil; the slow cracking of Helgrind's gates; the flicker of flame beneath Muspelheim's skin; the rise and fall of shadowed wings in Jötunheim's windless heights.

And far below, beneath the churn of waves — he saw it.

Naglfar. The ship of the dead, gliding like a wound made real. Its hull stitched from neglect. Its sail steeped in rot. And at its helm… the familiar flame.

"Loki," he whispered, the name falling like a stone into the deep. "So, we begin where we end."

One hand hovered near Gjallarhorn, its mouth chased with gold, its silence heavier than prophecy. It was the horn meant to call gods to their last war, the breath that would wake the world to ruin.

Heimdall did not raise it.

"Not yet," he murmured, eyes never blinking. "Let them hope. Let them breathe. One moment more."

The sky darkened around him. But Heimdall did not move. His golden armour caught the last true light of the Nine Realms. His stance — upright, unmoving — was a devotion carved into flesh.

He was the wall before the flood. The silence before the scream. The Watcher who would not blink, even when the stars fell.

And above him, the heavens held their breath. Waiting for the sound that would break them.

ᚠ

High upon Hliðskjálf, the seat from which all worlds could be seen, Odin All-Father sat unmoving.

The vaulted halls of Valaskjálf echoed only with wind, that thin and ancient breath that speaks when even gods fall silent.

Huginn and Muninn rested upon his shoulders — Thought and Memory — but neither stirred. Their wings were folded, their voices hushed. Even they knew: the age of questions had ended. The answer was coming.

Odin's one eye, sacrificed for wisdom, had seen much. He had hung nine nights upon the tree. He had bled for the runes that bound the very threads of fate. He had peered into Mímir's well and drunk of its secret sorrow.

And yet, all his knowledge, all his sacrifice, stood now like frost before fire.

Across the farthest sea, he watched the dark shape of Naglfar split the waves. Its hull, made of death, groaned like prophecy awakened. Its sail, black as mourning, fat with wind. At its helm burned vengeance in human form.

"Forged by dwarven hands, fated for mine," Odin said, voice like old bark cracking. "I spun the web, yet even I am caught within it. Let none speak of blame. Let them say what it was — my design. My war."

57

His gaze dropped to Gungnir, the spear that never misses. Its tip shimmered faintly with runes even he had forgotten how to read.

"I shall die with it in my hand," he whispered. "As I must."

But still, he did not rise. Not yet.

He sat beneath the weight of centuries, beneath the burden of every oath broken in the name of order. He watched the sea burn. He felt the tree shudder. He heard the silence of the gods, and the distant, gathering roar.

He was not afraid. But he understood, at last, the cost.

And beyond the golden roof of Valaskjálf, the sky began to bleed.

# Chapter 8
# The Horn That Woke the World

Heimdal stood alone.

At the farthest edge of Asgard, where sky kissed void and colour held the last line, he stood atop Bifröst—the burning bridge, the breath between realms.

It stretched beneath him in trembling light, that ancient arc of flame and frost, of colour and song, now dulled at its seams.

Red faded into violet. Gold bled into dusk. Each hue frayed like threads in a tapestry unravelling under unseen hands.

Beneath it yawned the chasm—Ginnungagap, deep and wordless.

Above, the stars held still, as if waiting to fall.

Heimdal did not move.

His ears, sharper than any blade, heard it all:

The frost-crack of Hel's host approaching from the north,

The slithering rot of death-laced boots on ice,

The clatter of ten thousand fingernails scratching the hull of Naglfar as it surged through blackened seas—each sound a drumbeat in the march to doom.

The bridge beneath him groaned—stone, fire, and light straining as if the cosmos itself flinched from what drew near.

His hand rested upon Gjallarhorn.

It pulsed faintly. Not yet sounded, but already awakened.

Its rim, cold as burial steel, gleamed with runes only the end would ever understand.

He knew: one breath into it, and every realm would hear.

Not just the living. Not just the gods.

But the dead, and those still unborn.

Heimdal's jaw clenched. His golden armour caught no reflection. There were no mirrors left in the world.

Behind him, the towers of Asgard flickered—not as a beacon, but as a candle caught in the wind of a coming storm.

He was the Watcher. The Guardian.

The eye at the edge.

The first to see the blade fall,

The last to be silenced.

Still, the horn remained at his side.

Not yet.

But the sky had begun to redden.

The sea had broken open.

And the bridge—Bifröst, beloved arc of unity—had begun to weep light.

One drop at a time.

ᛏ

In Vanaheim, where wildflowers once danced like firelight on water, where rivers laughed in the old tongue of the Vanir and barley bowed gold beneath an eternal sun—now, the fields had fallen silent.

The earth was pale, cracked like a broken oath.

No wind moved.

No birds sang.

Even the sun, once proud in its arc, sagged low on the horizon— not veiled by cloud, but heavy with grief.

Amid this dying garden, Freyr moved alone.

His feet whispered across frost-dusted grass.

In his hands, a rack of antlers, once part of a stag of the deep woods, swept the air in circles of silent defiance.

Low. High. Parry. Turn.

The forms flowed—flawless, measured, ancient. But each strike ended hollow. Each breath lingered too long.

The antlers were heavy with memory, yet weak for war.

They bore no fire. No prophecy.

They were not like the sword he had once carried.

He remembered it well:

A blade that blazed with its own will. Runes carved in sun-metal. A weapon worthy of gods.

A sword fated to strike against the flame-born king of Muspelheim.

But Freyr had given it away.

He saw her then—Gerðr, frost-daughter, storm-blooded. Her eyes had once been glacier stone.

Her voice, wind over ice.

When first they met, she would not look at him.

But when she finally did, winter melted in her gaze.

She reached out—

And spring awoke.

He had given the sword for her.

Not as ransom. As offering. As vow.

And now, the winter had returned to claim what love had delayed.

The antlers faltered in his grasp. Their tines dipped toward the earth.

He closed his eyes.

And from the bare-limbed trees, a voice whispered—soft, ancient, half memory, half fate:

"Will you face death with a beast's crown?"

Freyr pressed the tines to his brow.

The antlers warmed in his hands—slightly. As if remembering the life of the forest.

"No," he murmured.

"I will face it as I am—

not with flame,

not with steel,

but with the memory of love…

and the will to stand."

High atop Hliðskjálf, the throne that sees across the Nine Realms, Odin sat like the silence before a storm.

His one eye, dark with knowledge, blazed with the weight of what he had seen.

Not prophecy.

Reality.

From this seat above the sky, he looked upon a world unravelling:

In Jötunheim, fire bloomed among the ice-ridged crags like war-flowers, giants rising from sleep with fists of stone and frostbitten fury.

In Helheim, the gates groaned open, wide as the hunger of the grave. The dead stirred—silent legions sharpening centuries of scorn into blades.

On the seas of Niflheim, Naglfar cut its path through black water— its hull a spine, its ribs a cage of nailed bone, its sails fed by the breath of the forgotten.

And the sky began to bleed.

Odin did not flinch.

He turned from the great seeing, the winds behind him thick with the rustle of feathers.

Huginn and Muninn circled close—Thought and Memory, his last companions, now silent, now still.

Descending from Hliðskjálf into the hallowed silver depths of Valaskjálf, he walked beneath a roof that had once sung with laughter, now hushed as a tomb.

There, in the golden hush of twilight's end, he summoned the gods.

Those born of Asgard's light, and those long feasted in his hall.

The Einherjar came—heroes of forgotten wars, warriors whose names had become dust in mortal tongues.

Steel rang faintly at their sides, and death rode in their eyes like an old friend.

They came not for vengeance.

They came for duty.

They came for honour.

Thor was the first.

He strode into the hall like thunder walking—shoulders wide with storm, Mjölnir humming low, aching for the clash.

His brow was furrowed not with rage, but with resolve.

Eyes once full of laughter now burned with fate.

He did not kneel. He did not speak in riddles.

He only asked, with a voice like the wind beneath a gathering storm:

"It is time?"

Odin did not blink.

He nodded once—precise, final, full of centuries.

No more was said.

There was nothing left to plan.

The war they had long foreseen had stepped through the veil.

And the gods stood to meet it.

Frigg walked alone beneath the roots of Yggdrasil, her bare feet tracing paths worn by weeping time.

Her cloak dragged behind her, heavy with ash, heavy with memory.

Above, the light of the world had already faded.

Only shadows walked with her now.

She passed beneath branches that no longer sang in the wind. The leaves were black with grief, the bark split and weeping sap like old wounds reopened.

The great roots curled around her like the ribs of the world, narrowing with every step as she descended.

Down...

Down, where even gods must bow to what is written.

Down, to the place where sorrow is born.

At last, she came to Urðarbrunnr, the Well of Fate—its waters still and dark, untouched by time or mercy.

And there sat the Norns.

Urðr, unmoving, her face carved from silence.

Verðandi, her breath shallow, like a candle about to gutter.

Skuld, her eyes unreadable, her hand paused mid-thread.

They did not look at Frigg.

They did not speak.

They had seen her coming long before she chose to walk this path.

Frigg fell to her knees. The stone welcomed her like a tomb.

Her voice, when it came, cracked and raw:

"Please."

A single word. Too small for the grief it carried.

She lifted her head and whispered to the unmoving fates:

"Give him back. Or let me follow."

Her voice trembled like a broken harp string.

"He was the light in all our halls. My boy. My bright one."

The waters shimmered—but showed no vision.

No future. No mercy.

Only the reflection of a mother carved hollow by loss.

Tears slipped from her eyes—silent, ceaseless, like snow melting in spring.

They struck the stone in soft patters.

Not the regal weeping of a queen, but the broken sobs of a mother who had buried the sun.

Still, the Norns did not move.

"He should not be there," she cried.

"He did no wrong. I swore I would protect him. I begged the world to spare him. And still... still..."

Her hands gripped the hem of her cloak, nails digging into the fabric like claws.

"Do the fates not mourn? Do your threads feel nothing?"

But silence was the only answer—

a silence so deep it might have been the sound of the end itself.

And Frigg, goddess, queen, mother, bowed her head and wept.

She wept until her body could bear no more.

Until even the well seemed to hold its breath.

And when at last she rose—slow, unsteady—the water did not ripple.

The loom remained untouched.

The future unrevealed.

Urðarbrunnr remained blank.

A mirror too kind to show what comes next.

Or too cruel.

Frigg turned and left that place of silence behind.

But her grief remained, braided now into the roots of the world,

quiet and eternal—

a sorrow too deep for thread.

ᛏ

Naglfar cleaved the sea like a blade drawn across the throat of the world.

Its black hull, fashioned from the unburnt nails of the forgotten dead, cut through the waves without sound.

The ocean recoiled, unwilling to touch it.

No gulls followed. No wind dared sing.

It did not creak or groan—

It whispered.

A sound like bone breaking beneath ancient ice.

At its helm stood Loki.

He did not laugh.

Not now.

The salt wind coiled through his hair, now wild and red as a burning sky.

His eyes, once quick with mischief, burned with something colder—older.

His face was drawn, etched not by years but by torment remembered too clearly:

The serpent's venom, searing down his cheeks.

The iron taste of silence.

The scream of a son turned beast.

The warm spill of entrails, used not to bind him, but to erase him.

No chains wrapped him now.

And yet, he wore the memory of them in the way he stood—

back straight, jaw clenched, gaze fixed on the bleeding horizon.

Beside him stood Hel, his daughter, sovereign of the shadow realm. Her cloak trailed like smoke, her presence quiet as snowfall on a grave.

One half of her face was smooth, noble, unmarked by death.

The other, bone laid bare, smiling always.

She did not speak. She did not blink.

Before them rose Bifröst, the rainbow bridge, arcing in silence across the storm-stained sky.

Its colours were no longer bright with peace, but hard-edged and bleeding—

red into gold, blue into violet—

a blade drawn from light itself.

Loki's fingers gripped the helm. He closed his eyes and tasted the air: salt, rot, and prophecy.

"Heimdal waits," he murmured. "He always does."

Hel gave no answer. She had no need.

The ship surged forward.

Behind them stood an army of the dead—forgotten children, oath-breakers, mothers cast into silence, kings buried without song.

They did not shout. They did not beat shields.

They simply stood.

Still.

And together, they sailed toward judgement—

toward the shattering sky,

toward the bridge that still dared to shine,

toward the gods who had not yet paid.

Naglfar bore them not to battle,

but to reckoning.

High upon Bifröst, where the sky met the edge of all things, Heimdal stood still.

One hand rested upon the rainbow bridge, the other upon the horn that waits.

Gjallarhorn, silent since the dawn of time, now pulsed beneath his grip.

Carved from the marrow of the first giant, polished by sunfire, tempered in moonlight—it had never known mortal breath.

It waited only for this.

Heimdal, the Ever-Watchful, closed his eyes.

The moment stretched—tight as a bowstring, brittle as frost.

Time held its breath.

The wind died.

The seas stilled, their skin smooth as obsidian.

Leaves froze mid-fall.

Birds hung between wingbeats.

Even the stars dimmed,

as if afraid to see what must come.

And then—he blew.

Gjallarhorn sang.

Not a blast. Not a call. A shatter.

A sound like creation reversing.

Like mountains crumbling into dust.

Like fire weeping from the marrow of the void.

It split the sky.

It pierced the deepest tombs.

It cracked the silence beneath Hel's throne.

It stirred the embers at the heart of Muspelheim.

It reached every corner of the Nine Realms.

Children woke screaming, though they did not know why.

The old clutched their chests and wept for things forgotten.

The unborn twisted in the womb.

Even the gods flinched.

Yggdrasil groaned. Its roots twisted in pain.

Its branches rained sparks.

The Well of Urd boiled with memory.

In Asgard, golden halls fell silent.

The clash of sword on shield ceased.

Warriors, weavers, and seers stood motionless, as if breath itself had turned to frost.

Frigg, alone in Baldur's chamber, gripped the carved frame of her son's empty bed.

She whispered his name.

The wind stole it away.

Odin, within Valaskjálf's silver heights, clenched Gungnir in a white-knuckled grip.

The spear trembled, runes glowing faint with old oaths.

He did not rise—

But he would.

Soon.

In Vanaheim, the gardens groaned.

The fields split open, the wheat collapsed.

Freyr, mid-form, paused with antlers in hand.

A single tear rolled down his cheek—

Not for fear, but for the beauty he knew would burn.

Birds burst from the trees, their cries sharp as knives.

In Midgard, hearts clenched like fists.

Infants wailed.

Shepherds stared at the sky, mute.

Old feuds, long buried, flared like dry tinder.

In temples, prayers faltered.

In mead halls, songs died.

The wise turned their faces to the wind and whispered:

"The twilight has begun."

In Jötunheim, the ice cracked—groaning like ancient grief.

Eyes blinked open in the glacier walls, older than gods, colder than time.

Frost giants stirred, lifting spears the size of trees.

They did not speak.

They had waited.

In Muspelheim, flame soared high as the sky.

Surtr, Lord of Fire, stood from his basalt throne, fingers closing around the hilt of his sword.

Each footstep melted stone.

Each breath blackened the air.

His voice thundered:

"The hour is come. Let the world be cinders."

In Alfheim and Svartalfheim, elves turned silver faces toward the fading sun.

Their songs trembled.

Dwarves paused in their halls.

Hammer met anvil one last time—

Then silence.

Even gold lost its lustre.

And deep beneath it all...

In the cavern that once held the broken god, the scream returned.

The walls remembered.

The venom. The chains. The truth beneath the lies.

The chains now lay slack.

The cave stank of old pain.

The stone still echoed his name.

And above—

On the edge of the void—

Bifröst cracked.

Not yet broken.

But groaning.

Buckling beneath the weight of what marched toward it.

ᛏ

The Nine Realms Heard.

The sound did not fade.

It settled—in stone and in spirit, in root and in rune, in every breath drawn beneath the dome of the sky.

It burned through the branches of Yggdrasil, like fire licking dry leaves.

And across the Nine Realms, they answered.

The gods.

The dead.

The damned.

And all those who had waited too long in the dark.

# *Chapter 9*
# *No Signs but The Breaking Sky*

In the shadow of twilight, beneath the roots of Yggdrasil, Odin came once more to Mímir's Well.

The waters shimmered like memory, still and silver, untouched by wind or time. No ripple stirred.

No whisper rose.

Half-sunken in moss and frost, Mímir's head lay where Odin had left it—eyes closed, mouth sealed by silence.

The whisperer of ages, the voice of riddles, now mute.

Whether his wisdom was spent, or simply withheld, none could say.

Odin knelt.

From the folds of his cloak, he drew a single rune—carved long ago, on the day he first hung upon the Tree. Not a rune of death, but of ending. Not surrender, but the last thread of knowing. A truth too final for return.

He let it fall.

It touched the water with barely a sound—a kiss upon eternity, and sank without turning.

Odin's one eye followed it, the reflection of a world vanishing in its wake.

"So," he murmured, voice low as shifting earth, "even you are silent now."

The Well gave no answer.

No ripple. No echo.

He rose slowly, like a mountain remembering its burden.

There were no more riddles.

No more choices.

No prophecy to follow.

Only the path he had carved himself—

with blood, and loss, and unrelenting will.

He turned.

And behind him, the waters remained still.

Like a grave.

☦

Frigg returned to the hall of Asgard, her footsteps silent, her face carved from resolve.

She did not weep. Not now.

Her cloak was drawn close against the cold that no fire could banish—the chill that came not from winter, but from endings.

At the throne, she paused. She pressed a kiss to Odin's weathered cheek—light as breath, fierce as a vow. A promise whispered in the shadow of doom.

At the gates stood Thor, the storm given form. Mjölnir thrummed in his fist, lightning snarling around its head, each crackle a heartbeat of war.

His gaze burned with fury... but beneath the fire, grief coiled, heavy and quiet.

Freyr followed, bearing no sword.

In his hands, a stag's crown, tines worn smooth by time and tenderness.

He had traded steel for love.

And now, he would stand with empty hands against the fire, unflinching.

Tyr said nothing.

His one hand rested on his blade, the other long since taken in sacrifice.

He was justice without illusion. Honour made flesh.

Sif arrived like a golden flame, braiding her hair with calm precision—

not vanity, but ritual. A warrior's grace in the face of ruin.

Idunn came with no shield, no spear.

Only a pouch of her golden apples—seeds of life, carried into death.

Her presence was not for battle, but for memory. For renewal, should the world survive.

And far above, where the bridge touched sky, Heimdal stood sentinel.

His hand curled around Gjallarhorn, its note still echoing in the bones of the world.

Tears had long since dried on his cheeks.

What remained was duty—pure, unblinking, absolute.

Together they waited.

A host of gods, fewer than in ages past.

Stronger in silence than in song.

Bound not by victory, but by resolve.

And above them, the sky trembled.

This was the stillness before the storm.

The breath before the world shattered.

ᛏ

Naglfar surged from the mist like a wound torn into the sea.

Its hull gleamed with the sheen of frost and death; black timbers stitched from the unburned nails of the forgotten. It sailed not by wind nor oar, but by the will of the dead—those denied rest, those who had no songs sung over their graves. Their grief was the tide. Their vengeance, the current.

Their whispers filled the sails.

At the base of Bifröst, the rainbow bridge groaned.

Not the groan of wood or stone—

But of a spine breaking.

Of a world that had carried too much for too long.

From Naglfar's prow, Loki raised his head.

The shifting colours of the bridge shimmered in the burn-scarred hollows of his face. He said nothing.

He didn't need to.

At the apex stood Heimdal, golden-armoured, unmoved. One hand rested on Gjallarhorn, the other clenched at his side. A crack hissed beneath his feet—thin as a thread, glowing red as ruin.

His white eyes flicked toward it, calm, unblinking.

Beside him strode Thor, Mjölnir humming with storm-song,

sparks hissing from the head of the hammer like fireflies seeking blood.

Odin came last.

The wind recoiled from him. His cloak billowed like thunderclouds torn loose from the sky.

In his hand, Gungnir, the spear that never missed, etched with runes older than fate.

He did not look at Loki.

He looked at the crack.

And Freyr, gentle Freyr, stepped to the line.

No steel in his grip—only a stag's crown, pale and sure.

He knew it would splinter like brittle bone.

He held it anyway.

The air stilled. Above, the sky dimmed, stars blinking out one by one.

Below, the roots of Yggdrasil stirred and shuddered like something roused from a thousand-year sleep.

No birds sang. No winds danced.

The world waited.

Then from behind Naglfar came the giants.

From Jötunheim, the old enemies.

They rose like moving mountains, ice clinging to their flesh,

fire bleeding from their mouths.

They did not roar. They did not bellow.

They marched in silence, the silence of inevitability.

Heimdal's jaw tightened. His hand gripped the horn. The bridge beneath him pulsed—once, twice—like a dying heart.

And then...

A crack bloomed beneath him—golden, jagged, alive.

It ran like fire through silk, racing toward the sea.

The gods did not speak.

They did not run.

They watched as the sky fractured, as Bifröst, the bridge of all realms, the arc of connection between God and mortal, shivered…

…then shattered.

And the fall began.

### <u>The Last Song of the Gods</u>

*They rode to doom with open eyes,*

*Beneath a bleeding, broken sky.*

*No coward fled, no oath betrayed,*

*Each met the end the Norns had made.*

*Yet echo lingers, strong and wide,*

*In thunder's roll and ocean's tide.*

*For though their flesh to flame was cast,*

*The stories sung shall ever last.*

# Chapter 10
# *Ragnarök*

Vígríðr stretched beyond all reckoning, a wasteland of ash and splintered stone.

Nothing grew, nothing stirred.

The sky sagged beneath storm clouds, and even the wind dared not breathe.

Odin sat astride Sleipnir, a silhouette of stillness amid the dying world.

His wolves circled, restless. His ravens wheeled above, uneasy.

He said, not to his warriors but to fate itself, "This is the place. Where everything ends."

Behind him, the gods came forth like dawn rising through ruin:

Thor, grim and red-bearded, Mjölnir crackling in his fist, storm-light in his eyes.

Freyr, swordless but resolute, stag's antlers at his side—no weapon, but a vow.

Tyr, teeth clenched, his sword gripped one-handed, the other lost to a wolf's betrayal.

Heimdall, ever-watchful, Gjallarhorn silent at his belt, gaze fixed on the horizon.

Sif, her hair bound in golden braids, axe kissed with fire.

Idunn, quiet, clutching a single pouch of apples—life in the face of doom.

Freyja, cloaked in falcon-feathers, eyes burning with the fury of a mother goddess.

And behind them, not gods—but mortals.

From Midgard they came. Old warriors and younger fools, shield-maidens and seers, farmers who

once lit candles to Odin, children who learned the runes not as prayers but as survival.

Some wore rusted mail. Others cloaks of fur and bone.

They had lived through the long winters. They had watched the sky grow still.

Now, they marched beside their gods—not for victory, but for memory. For honour.

From the east, the sea opened like a wound.

Naglfar rose from its depths, its hull stitched from the unburied nails of the dead.

It keened, a dirge on the wind.

Its black sail billowed with the breath of the forgotten.

At the prow stood Loki, hair tangled like storm clouds, eyes blazing with fire long buried.

Around him gathered the legions of the end:

Frost giants, flesh cracked with ice, eyes like frozen moons.

Fire-born, wreathed in ash and ember, with Surtr at their head, his blade a sun of ruin.

The dead of Hel, not heroes but the denied—kings buried without name.

Women drowned for shame. Oath-breakers, plague-bearers, forgotten multitudes unwept.

And above them came Loki's monstrous blood:

Hel, veiled in mist, her voice like snowfall on bone.

Jörmungandr, rising in spirals from the deep, his breath blackening the sky.

Fenrir, terrible and vast, jaws parted wide enough to swallow the sun.

"It is time, Father," growled the wolf.

Loki stepped onto the ash-blown earth, the air buckled around him, heat and sorrow.

"Let the world burn," he said.

Behind him, the host moved like a wound across the plain.

And across from them, the gods stood—motionless, waiting.

But not alone.

The mortals of Midgard raised their spears. Some with trembling hands. Some with none at all.

But their eyes held steady.

Thor lifted Mjölnir.

Heimdall reached for his blade.

Odin lowered his spear.

"Let it begin," he whispered.

A hush fell—not the hush of peace, but of everything holding its breath.

Time slowed.

The wind froze.

Ash hung still in the air.

Even sound dared not tread across the silence.

Odin and Loki, once blood-brothers, now stood as symbols—Order and Chaos.

Sacrifice and rage. A crown of wolves and a crown of wounds.

Their eyes met.

Odin's gaze was storm-dark, sorrowful, resigned.

Loki's burned—rage, betrayal, and a justice no god had granted.

Above them, Huginn and Muninn circled once, then turned…

…and flew away.

A snowflake fell.

It caught the faint light, shimmered for one heartbeat—and vanished before touching earth.

Thor shifted his grip.

Freyr traced his fingers over old runes.

Tyr clenched his jaw, his phantom hand aching with memory.

Freyja narrowed her eyes.

Sif braced her stance.

Idunn pressed her apples to her chest.

Among the mortal ranks, a mother whispered to her son, "We stand where the old songs end."

He nodded. "Then let us be the verse they remember."

Across the plain, Fenrir snarled.

Jörmungandr hissed.

The fire-giants lifted their blades.

Hel raised her skeletal hand.

No one moved. Not yet.

Then…

The sky rumbled.

Odin lowered his spear.

Loki took one step forward.

And the world tore into war.

Before the gods moved, the mortals ran.

They did not march like legions.

They did not wait for command.

They charged like waves against a storm.

Men and women of Midgard, once scattered clans and shattered kingdoms, now stood shoulder to shoulder.

No prophecy compelled them.

No god demanded their sacrifice.

They came of their own will—to fight beside the divine, to die on their feet, to be remembered.

A king from the North raised his axe skyward, its edge red with runes.

A shield-maiden from the East screamed a war cry that cracked the air like thunder.

A boy—barely more than a child—ran forward, tears streaming on his cheeks, blade shaking in his hand.

They hurled themselves at death, not for glory, but for memory.

They drove bronze and elm into the frost giants; their faces twisted with fear and unyielding fire.

They clashed with Hel's dead legions—steel meeting rot, spirit meeting silence.

They held the line as fire-giants scorched the sky, as ash fell like snow, as their banners turned to flame and smoke.

Blood darkened the snow. Screams mingled with roars. And still—they fought.

One by one, they fell.

But not before striking.

Not before being seen.

And the gods saw.

From the heart of the storm, Odin rode forth.

Sleipnir's hooves beat thunder into the bones of the world. Ash curled in his wake. His cloak trailed like the shadow of an age. Silver-threaded, battle-worn, and clasped with a pin. The All-Father entered.

And before him stood Fenrir.

The great wolf.

The devourer.

His fur was matted with ice and flame, his breath the rot of ruin, his jaws gaping wide enough to drown the sun.

He snarled once—a sound that cracked the air and shivered the roots of Yggdrasil—and leapt.

Odin did not flinch.

Gungnir flew.

The spear that never missed, singing with runes, struck true—

But Fenrir twisted, blood spraying across the battlefield like ink on prophecy.

The wolf howled, a sound that tore through the Nine Realms like the scream of creation dying.

And then—he struck.

Teeth met God.

Sleipnir fell.

Odin was torn from the saddle, slammed into the earth. The ground split beneath them.

A quake of God and beast.

Stone shattered.

Dust rose like the breath of the world.

Odin rolled, rising.

He stood—tall. Steady. Silent.

His eye—blazing.

His grip—sure.

His voice—none.

There were no words left.

Only the spear.

Gungnir flashed again.

Fenrir staggered.

Wounded. But not slain.

He circled.

The wolf and the god.

The chain-breaker and the wisdom-seeker.

One born to destroy.

One born to know.

The god who had once hung for knowledge.

The god who had given everything for foresight.

Now stood before fate—with nothing left but will.

Behind them, the storm of war roared.

The gods bled and the mortals burned.

And the wolf's jaws widened once more.

Thor saw Fenrir strike—and roared.

The storm broke with him.

The heavens cracked as he surged upward, Mjölnir alight with the fury of ten thousand thunders. He soared like wrath itself and came down upon Jörmungandr, the World Serpent, whose coils split the sea and slithered across the plain like a river of doom.

Thunder met poison. Lightning crowned his hammer and lit the serpent's scales like burning oil. The sky turned white.

Every strike from Thor sent tremors through Yggdrasil. Every lash of the serpent's tail carved canyons through stone and bone.

Above them, the clouds bled fire.

Below, the roots of the world screamed.

Elsewhere, Freyr met Surtr.

A god of summer, face to face with the flame of the end.

In Freyr's hands: only a stag's crown, tines etched with runes of peace.

Against Surtr's sword, forged in fire before fire had a name.

Still, Freyr stood, and when antler met flame, the sky ignited.

They fought beneath a rain of stars turned to ash.

Freyja streaked across the field like a falcon unchained, her falcon cloak snapping like wings of war.

She danced between beasts and giants, her spear red with ruin, her braids undone, her voice a shriek of battle and grief.

She struck with love. She struck with rage.

And behind her came the shield-maidens of Vanaheim, screaming oaths older than the Æsir.

Tyr, the one-handed god, plunged into the dead ranks of Hel.

Undone warriors. Mothers still in burial linen. Children with blades of bone.

He met them all with steel and silence.

Sword in one hand, justice in the hollow where the other once had been.

He did not falter.

Each blow was a vow fulfilled.

Each cut, a confession.

And Heimdall—the Watcher, eyes bright as suns.

Sword drawn from silence.

He turned from the ruined sky and ran. Toward Loki.

The Trickster waited with his knives of wind and shadow; a smile split like a scar across his face.

They met at the edge of the bridge that no longer stood.

The beginning had returned to the beginning.

Their blades met like thunderclaps.

Heimdall, guardian of the bridge, stood radiant in his golden armour, every step measured, every strike a truth forged in silence.

His sword shone with the light of the Nine Realms, a blade not meant for war, but for the reckoning that ends it.

Loki moved like shadow set loose, his dagger curved like mockery, like memory turned cruel.

His laughter rang out, bitter as ash.

"You always watched, Heimdall," he sneered between strikes, blades flashing. "But you never saw me."

"I saw enough," Heimdall answered, his voice steady as stone.

Steel screamed. Sparks bled into flame.

Loki lunged low, swift as smoke. Heimdall blocked, twisted, drove him back.

Blood followed—one drop tracing down Loki's brow, one blooming from Heimdall's side.

They circled, breath ragged, eyes locked.

Dust coiled around them. Firelight danced.

Two ancient truths.

One born to guard.

One born to betray.

And in the ruin of the world, they met, first and last. Watcher and Trickster.

Both knowing neither would walk away.

The mortals held the ruined line.

Men and women, young and old, stood shoulder to shoulder in the ashes of the world.

Against the tide of giants, beasts, and dead things, they braced themselves—not with hope, but with defiance.

A war-chanted shield wall rose, roaring its answer to the end of days.

Screams split the air. Bones cracked like splintering ice.

Fire rained from above, turning soil to black glass and breath to steam.

The sky had forgotten light—only smoke remained, churning and endless.

But still, they did not break.

A wounded jarl, one eye swollen shut, his face broken and bleeding, stood atop the corpse of a frost giant and bellowed through blood-choked teeth,

"HOLD! HOOOLD!"

Beside him, a priestess of Freyr knelt in the ash, dragging a dying warrior from the flames. Her robes smouldered. Her hands shook.

But her lips moved still—soft prayers to a god whose fields would never bloom again.

Children too young for swords gripped torches, hurled stones.

One boy, no older than ten, tied his dead brother's belt around his waist like armour.

Mothers screamed the names of sons already gone.

A father held his daughter's broken body, then rose with her blade in hand,

his tears lost to the soot.

Some sang songs old as stone, old as starlight—

raw, broken-throated hymns rising over the clash of metal and monster.

They were not gods.

They had no runes.

No relics.

Only flesh.

Only fury.

And the gods saw.

From the edge of Vígríðr, Thor turned as a band of warriors locked shields around a wounded woman, guarding her as she lit a torch and cast it at an ice giant's feet.

The beast howled, staggered, then fell.

Tyr, soaked in black blood, watched a limping archer fire her last arrow into a giant's throat—

and smiled.

The shield wall trembled.

It bled.

It burned.

But it did not yield.

And for that, the gods themselves drew breath.

⸸

The sea boiled. Waves the height of mountains slammed against the broken coast. Salt and blood churned in the froth.

And from the deep, the coil of Jörmungandr rose.

His body encircled the world—vast as the horizon, slick with poison.

Scales black as void shattered the surface like rising reefs.

Lightning tore the sky, and in its stuttering flash, the serpent's head lifted above the storm.

Eyes like twin abyssal moons locked onto the shore.

And Thor came.

The storm walked with him. Thunder at his heels, lightning in his bones.

He strode down the shattered cliffs where gods and mortals lay broken,

Mjölnir crackling with rage in his grip.

Rain washed his face. Blood mingled with it. His braids hung heavy with seawater and battle—but his stride did not falter.

The Midgard Serpent reared higher.

Its maw opened wide, revealing fangs like glacial spires, venom streaming down in torrents.

The tide sizzled where it struck—stone cracked, bone dissolved.

Thor did not speak.

The time for words had drowned with the sun.

He hurled Mjölnir.

The hammer screamed through the dark, a streak of fury and flame,

and struck the serpent's skull with a crack like the sky breaking open.

Jörmungandr roared.

The sea surged forward, swallowing the shore, dragging corpses and fire into the deep.

Thor leapt.

Into the heart of the storm. Into the serpent's fury.

Unblinking. Unbowed.

They met where sky and sea blurred into chaos.

The thunder god and the world-serpent.

Clashing beneath the storm.

Mjölnir rose—again, again—striking scale, fang, muscle, myth.

Jörmungandr twisted—coils shattering cliffs, tail lashing mountains to rubble.

Venom fell in sheets, turning waves to black steam.

The air cracked like brittle ice beneath the hammer's howl.

The sea heaved and split.

The battlefield paused.

Gods and men turned their heads to the clash at the edge of the world.

And then—

from across the plain, another cry rose.

In the heart-shadow of the battlefield, where smoke veiled the sun and ash rained like snow, the Einherjar held their ground.

Surtr loomed—a mountain of molten flesh, crowned in flame, his every step branding the earth.

In his hand, the sword of the end—a blade born before the stars, glowing with the heat of the first spark and the last silence.

The air around it trembled.

Reality bent.

They stood armoured, shields raised, spears and axes ready. No single god, no single hero could turn back this tide. Only unity, courage, and the stubborn defiance of mortal valour.

Surtr swung. The fire howled.

The sword split the ground—craters bloomed where it passed.

The Einherjar moved as one—a storm of iron and will. They weaved between the strikes, their shields a lattice against flame, their spears striking in measured rhythm. They fought not with wrath, but with memory, with honour, with the weight of those who had fallen before them.

For a breath—they turned back the tide of fire.

For a breath.

But fire cannot be stopped.

It is patient. It is cruel. It consumes.

Surtr roared, and the sky blazed.

Shields splintered. Spears shattered.

They fell beneath the blaze, consumed in fire and ash.

The sky darkened as the ash drifted like snow.

ᛏ

Two figures faced one another—one cloaked in black, crowned with ravens; the other, a beast born of endings, his fur matted with blood, his breath steaming like forge-smoke.

Odin gripped Gungnir. The spear gleamed cold and true.

Fenrir's eyes burned like coals in the heart of a dying world.

His growl rumbled through the bones of the earth.

Then—he lunged.

Gungnir flew—a streak of divine will—striking deep beneath the wolf's shoulder.

Blood spilled, black and steaming.

But Fenrir did not fall.

Odin stepped forward.

He did not falter.

He met the beast head-on.

Claws flashed.

Teeth split the air.

The world held its breath.

Then they collided—a sound like a mountain breaking.

Sleipnir reared and vanished into the chaos.

The ground split wide.

Giants stumbled. Mortals fell.

Lightning tore the sky open.

Fenrir's jaws opened—impossibly wide—and then snapped shut.

Silence.

A single crack echoed across the plain—not storm. Not steel. But bone.

The gods turned.

The dead stood still.

Even the wind seemed to forget its path.

Odin was gone.

Only the ravens circled—crying, sharp and broken—as a single feather drifted down into the ash.

And Fenrir stood—steaming, bloodstained, the last of the Allfather's breath still warm upon his fangs.

Above, the sky bled red.

The centre of the world had fallen. And the battle had only just begun.

ᛏ

They came in a blaze of gold and blood.

Freyja led from the front—cloak of falcon feathers torn by fire, cheeks streaked with ash, not flying but running, sword in hand, boots pounding the burning earth.

Around her surged the war-band of Sessrúmnir—shield-maidens and reavers, berserkers and seers.

Some wore chainmail, some wore animal skins, others nothing but paint and fury.

They fought with axes carved from meteoric iron, with spears tipped in boar-tusk and prophecy.

These were not the calm, courtly dead of Valhalla—

they were Freyja's chosen. Lovers of beauty, devotees of death.

They struck Hel's horde like lightning over a barrow.

Half-rotted warriors stumbled forward, only to be torn down by shrieking Valkyries.

A withered king, crowned with rust, raised his ancient blade—and Freyja herself cut him down.

Her sword blazed like a ribbon of flame in the dusk.

Beside her, Brynja, a warrior-priestess, sang as she fought—a song of love turned bitter.

Her blade moved like moonlight, and with every kill, she wept.

"Strike!" Freyja cried, her voice cutting through ash and agony. "Strike, and let the dead know they were not the only ones wronged!"

A man with no name, his face hidden behind a painted elk-skull, raised a torch to a mound of corpses and turned the battlefield to firelight.

The war-band surged—not for law, not for order, but for vengeance.

But the dead did not break.

They kept coming—row upon row, some still bearing the arrows that killed them, others dragging shattered limbs through mud and flame.

Among them moved Hel's handmaidens, cloaked in ice, whispering doom.

And Freyja—Freyja screamed back, louder than fate, her sword lifted to the storm-lit sky.

Týr walked alone into the tide of the dead.

He said no prayer. He gave no war cry.

His sword was drawn. His jaw set. And the empty sleeve at his shoulder fluttered like a torn banner in the wind.

Hel's army surged to meet him—spear-wielding corpses, wights with glowing eyes, drowned men dragging rusted chains behind them.

But they slowed.

Even the dead remembered the god who fed his hand to justice.

Týr cut through them with precise, brutal grace. Each stroke carved silence into the shrieking swarm. His blade burned not with magic, but with purpose.

There was no rage.

No fire.

Only resolve.

A corpse lunged with a shattered halberd—Týr stepped aside, struck once, and the thing collapsed like rotted timber.

A skeletal archer loosed a barbed arrow—he caught it in his scarred arm, let it tear through flesh, and kept walking.

Then came the kings—a ring of them.

Fallen monarchs, their bones wrapped in burial gold, their eyes aglow with ancient hatred.

They raised their blades in silence.

Not out of cruelty.

But reverence.

Týr raised his sword, met their gaze, and stepped forward.

Not far from the battlefield's heart, nestled in a hollow of birch and stone, stood one of the last sacred groves of the nine realms.

Here, the old prayers had once been spoken.

Here, offerings had hung like fruit from the branches.

And here—on the final day—a circle of mortals made their stand.

A grey-haired woman, once a seeress, stood barefoot in the snow. Chalk symbols marked her chest, and in her trembling hands she held a copper bowl filled with blood and herbs.

She sang, her voice cracked and raw.

Around her stood a dozen warriors—old men, boys, crippled veterans.

One bore no eyes, swinging a rusted sword at ghosts he could not see.

Another limped on a shattered leg bound to a pine-splint, gripping his spear in both hands.

"We hold here," said their leader, a one-eyed huntsman cloaked in wolfskins.

"If we fall, let it be at the roots of what still matters."

They did not speak again.

The dead came.

Where the corrupted brushed the birch trees, the bark split and bled black.

But the mortals did not run.

They fought.

With hatchets and staves.

With teeth and song.

With grief and memory.

The blind man screamed and swung.

The seeress poured the bowl over the roots and called to the Vanir with her dying breath.

A boy climbed a stone and drove a dagger into the face of a corpse that wore his father's smile.

And though they were dying, they held.

✝

The ring of dead kings lay broken, shattered beneath Týr's blade.

The god of justice stood alone, breath heaving, arm slick with the ichor of a thousand wights.

His sword was chipped to ruin. His one good hand bled.

Then came the growl—low, rolling, older than the gods.

From the mist rose Garmr, the Hound of Hel.

Chains still clung to his neck, broken links from a prison long shattered.

His fur dripped with blood and ash.

His eyes burned with corpse-fire.

His breath steamed with the rot of the underworld.

Týr's gaze did not waver.

They had always been fated to meet.

The beast lunged.

Týr roared and met the charge. Steel flashed.

He sidestepped the first strike—barely—and drove his blade deep into Garmr's shoulder.

The hound howled, jaws snapping wide—wide enough to swallow the sky—and struck.

Fangs tore into Týr's side.

He screamed—but he did not fall.

With his last strength, he drove the sword again, deep into Garmr's heart, twisting with fury, with finality.

The hound thrashed. Yelped. And stilled.

But the bite held fast.

Blood poured from Týr's mouth as he sank to one knee, then both.

His blade slipped from his hand.

He leaned forward, pressed his brow to the beast he had slain—a gesture not of hate, but of grim respect.

And there, locked in death with the guardian of Hel, Týr fell.

They came not in thunder, but in silence. Freyja walked at the front, barefoot on scorched ground, her falcon helm lowered over tearless eyes. Around her neck hung Brísingamen, dulled by ash and blood, yet pulsing faintly with the last light of lost Vanir magic.

Behind her moved the Daughters of Dusk, warriors robed in twilight hues. They carried curved blades, carved antler bows, and torches that burned with cold fire. They did not shout. They did not boast. They whispered oaths to the dead. Each had buried someone. Each had waited for this.

They moved through the battlefield like a tide of shadow and starlight, past broken men and burning banners, past the corpses of frost giants and fire-wreathed beasts, and towards the ranks of Hel's army. And when they struck, they gave no warning. No charge. No war cry. Only sudden violence.

Freyja moved like a storm behind a veil. Her seax flashed once, twice, thrice, and three draugr collapsed wordless at her feet. She slipped past a giant's downward blow and opened its throat with a motion no faster than breath.

"Don't look away," she said to no one. "Let the dead see who we are."

A mother of five buried her sickle in a corpse's chest, whispering her daughter's name. A hunter loosed an arrow into a giant's ribs and exhaled a satisfied sigh before drawing another.

These warriors did not fight for Asgard. They fought for memory, for the quiet places buried beneath ash, for names no skald would ever sing again. And when the sky cracked with lightning and fire, their eyes did not flinch.

They were not fury. They were reckoning.

The sea heaved like a dying beast. Waves the height of mountains battered the bloodstained cliffs. Salt stung the air. And from the abyss, the serpent rose. Jörmungandr, the world's girdle, fate given flesh, breached the deep like a living continent. Cascading tides fell from its back in waterfalls. Its scales, black as obsidian oil, caught no light. Each shift of its vast body churned the ocean into whirlpools. Where it rose, the horizon ended.

But thunder answered. Thor came with the storm at his heels. He was not merely a god now; he was the last storm. Rain carved lines through the blood on his face. His hair clung to his shoulders. The air hummed with the power of lightning not yet loosed. Mjölnir sparked in his grip. No words passed his lips. The time for oaths had passed. Only death remained.

The serpent reared its skull, vast enough to eclipse the sun, and spewed venom thick as tar. It fell like burning rain, searing stone and bone alike. Thor did not flinch. He hurled Mjölnir. The hammer tore through the storm, a streak of divine fury, and struck Jörmungandr's brow. The sky split with the sound of continents weeping. The serpent screamed, and the sea fled backward, the world recoiling from the clash of god and monster.

Then Thor leapt. He rose like a lightning bolt, arcing through smoke and ruin, and met the serpent in the air. They collided— storm and scale, order and chaos, shattering the cliffside and collapsing mountains into the sea. They crashed through wave and wreckage. Mjölnir rose and fell like the heartbeat of the world. Fangs like glacier spires tore through clouds. Each blow shook the Nine Realms. Venom met thunder. Poison hissed in Thor's blood, but still he struck.

From distant hills, mortals watched. One dropped to his knees. Another turned his eyes away. For what they witnessed was not war, it was the death of gods.

And then, through the maelstrom, came the final blow. Thor drove Mjölnir into the serpent's skull with such force that the sky forgot how to thunder. Jörmungandr writhed, the coils of fate unravelling. It screamed once more, a sound that cracked Yggdrasil's limbs, and then it collapsed, lifeless, into the sea it once encircled.

Thor staggered back. Once. Twice. Nine steps he took, each one a sacred toll, as if unmaking the Nine Realms with every stride. His blood boiled with poison. The venom that unmade worlds coiled inside him. And on the ninth step, he fell. Not in rage. Not in glory. But with silence, as the last storm passed from the sky.

ᚠ

As Thor fell beside the coiled corpse of Jörmungandr, the sky above split—not with thunder, but with silence. The air itself held its breath.

Then—howling.

From the far reaches of the firmament came two shadows, faster than wind, more ancient than the gods. Sköll, with fur of firelight and breath like a forge, chased the sun's chariot across the vast sky. Hati, lean and cold, streaked behind the moon's silver arc, frost clinging to his flanks.

Since the birth of time, they had pursued. Now, at the end of all things, they closed the distance. With jaws gaping wider than any mortal scream, Hati struck first. His teeth pierced moonlight. The silver orb shattered like glass. Shards fell like pale tears through the dark.

A heartbeat later, Sköll pounced, dragging the sun from the sky in a blaze of gold and ash. Fire spilled across the clouds. Light flared—and vanished.

Day and night were swallowed whole. The world fell into true twilight. Not dusk. Not dawn. A realm between heartbeats, between hope and horror.

And still, the wolves howled—no longer with hunger, but with victory.

⚡

The warriors of Midgard faltered. Axes wavered. Spears drooped. A boy no older than sixteen looked up from the corpse of his brother, blinking into the sudden dark. "What happened?" he whispered. "Where is the sun?"

A shield-maiden, smeared with soot, dropped to her knees, her blade buried in the gut of a frost giant. "It's gone," she said. "The sky is dead."

All across the plain, mortals turned their faces upward—and saw nothing. No sun. No moon. Only smoke. Only fire. And stars—now weeping embers in a drowning sky.

A jarl, blood running from a dozen wounds, roared to his men, "Do not break! Do not run! Let the gods see that we stood!"

They answered not with words, but by lifting shields once more. Even in the dark, they burned with defiance. And in that terrible, gods-forsaken silence... they charged again.

⚡

The battlefield was fire and ash. Frost clashed with flame. Bones shattered beneath giant boots. The sky had turned to cinder. And through the ruin came a sound—not of drums, nor horns, but of hooves, fast and furious.

104

Freyja rode at the head of her warband. Her cloak tore behind her like a banner of fire. Blood streaked her golden armour, and her falcon-feathered helm caught the last sparks of light. No longer the lover. No longer the sorceress. No longer the chooser of the slain. Now she was only the blade.

Around her rode her shield-sisters—warrior-women of the Vanir, faces streaked with war paint and grief. Some wept as they rode. Others sang—shrill, wild songs that made the dead turn their heads. They charged not to win, but to wound. Through the ranks of Hel's shambling dead they tore, cleaving corpses like rotted wood. Spear points danced like fireflies. Arrows howled like wolves.

Freyja herself cut down a frost giant with a strike that split its skull from crown to collarbone. "FOR LIFE!" one screamed. "FOR THE DEAD!" cried another. "FOR THE VANIR!" came the final roar.

And behind them, the world cracked. Surtr's shadow rose on the horizon. The fire giant moved like a mountain aflame, sword high, ready to sweep all things into ash. Freyja looked to the end. She turned to her sisters.

"We do not yield," she said. "We burn."

And with blades lit by their last fury, they charged again—into fire, into legend.

ᛏ

The sky bled ash. Smoke unfurled like torn banners across the ruin of Vígríðr. The clash of gods and monsters had become distant, faded to echoes behind walls of fire and dust. Here, where shadows thickened, Víðarr walked alone.

He had not wept. He had not screamed. He had not spoken. He was the silent one, the god forgotten in tales, the one who waited. His sorrow was not a flood. It was stone, buried deep, unmoved by time. Yet now, the earth itself knew his grief.

He stepped over bodies: gods, mortals, beasts. Through broken shields and shattered blades. He did not look for Fenrir. He knew where the beast would be. He had always known.

And then he saw it—the great wolf, its flanks heaving with the blood of gods, its fur clotted with fire, its eyes still glowing with the madness of slaughter. Odin's blood dripped from its fangs.

Víðarr stopped. No wind moved. No crow cried. No horn sounded. He stepped forward, one slow foot after another. With each stride, the memory of his father's death burned brighter. But he did not let rage take him. His silence was heavier than fury.

Upon his foot was the great shoe, woven not in haste, but gathered through the ages, from the cast-off leathers of all the Nine Worlds. The forgotten pieces. The discarded remnants. It was a thing of quiet preparation, crafted in patience. No boast had ever named it. No saga had sung of it. Yet it had waited, just as he had.

The wolf snarled—a thunderous, guttural sound that shook the stones. It lunged. But Víðarr surged in, driving his foot down upon its jaw, crushing it to the blood-soaked ground. The world reeled.

With both hands, he gripped the wolf's upper jaw. Muscles coiled like the roots of Yggdrasil itself. The beast thrashed. The ground split beneath them. Lightning tore the sky open. And with one terrible sound, part howl, part sundering, Víðarr tore Fenrir's skull apart.

The scream that followed was not only the wolf's. It was the scream of a world watching fate defied. Blood poured like a river. The wolf convulsed, once, twice, and then was still.

Víðarr stood above it, breath ragged. Not in triumph. Not in rage. Only in grief. He did not fall to his knees. He did not cry out his father's name. He simply looked toward the ruined stars falling in the smoke-choked sky...

...and waited for the next shadow to rise.

ᛏ

For the span of a single breath, all things held still. The battlefield—once a roaring sea of screams and steel—froze. Blades halted mid-swing. Fire hung motionless in the air. The shriek of a dying man faded into silence.

Because Fenrir was dead.

Across Vígríðr, warriors turned their heads—mortals and gods alike. They saw the great wolf, broken and still, his blood steaming across the cracked earth. And they saw Víðarr: lone, unmoving, standing like a monument to a justice older than time. Even the sky seemed to draw breath.

Near the grove, a shield-maiden dropped to her knees. "He's done it," she whispered, her voice lost in the wind. A fire giant stumbled, eyes wide. One of Hel's dead faltered, the echo of their master's fall bleeding into their bones. For the first time, doubt touched the enemy ranks.

But only for a moment. Fate, though cracked, was not undone. The darkness had not ended. And the gods knew it.

As the silence shattered—the battle roared back to life.


Beneath a sky torn open by fire, the world itself seemed to scream. Surtr strode across the blackened plain, his blade a star dragged from the heavens. Each step melted stone. His eyes were twin furnaces. His mouth exhaled ruin. He was not anger. He was ending made flesh.

Across from him stood Freyr. He bore no sword—only the cracked beast's antlers, scarred and heavy, marked with runes of peace, love, and summer's bloom. They were not meant for war. But neither was Freyr, until now. The god of fertility, of sunlit fields and laughing streams, stood defiant before the doom of flame.

Surtr spoke no words. The time for speeches had turned to cinders. He raised his sword.

Freyr charged. Ash flew with each step. Their clash echoed like thunder cracking the spine of the world. Freyr struck with the speed of wind over barley. His antlers battered Surtr's arm, deflecting the first sweep of that sun-forged blade. They held—for a moment. Then splintered like brittle bone in fire.

Surtr's next blow tore the sky open and sent Freyr to his knees. But even broken, Freyr rose once more—bleeding, burned, and laughing through bloodied teeth.

"For love, I gave my sword," he rasped. "Let that love be the last light you see."

He lunged. The beast's antlers tore into Surtr's side, goring through flame and flesh. The fire giant bellowed, staggering—not stopped, not slain, but marked. Blood and fire poured together, searing the wound so it would never close. And though Freyr knew his end was upon him, he had left his mark, carved deep as a hunter fells a stag.

Surtr howled—not in pain, but in wrath. Then, with a final swing, the fire-sword cleaved Freyr from the world. His blood steamed upon the soil. The green he had summoned withered. The sun god fell.

Surtr stood victorious. Then he turned to the sky.


At the broken span of Bifröst, where rainbow shards lay like glass upon ash, two figures stood.

Loki—the fire-eyed wanderer, no longer laughing. Venom had seared his skin. His blade, jagged and black, dripped with old spite. Shadows clung to him like smoke, as if the world itself recoiled.

Heimdall—the last sentinel, clad in scorched gold. His sword still gleamed with the light of a world not yet dead. His horn had been sounded, its cry lost to the void. There was nothing left to warn of. Nothing left to wait for.

They faced each other beneath a sky without stars. There were no words. Words had long since failed.

They moved. Blades clashed—prophecy colliding with memory. Every strike was known before it landed, not by sight, but by fate. For from the first breath of the cosmos, these two had been bound—

The Guardian of the Gods.

The Breaker of Bonds.

The end had always waited for their meeting.

Heimdall's breath was iron. Loki's was flame. One fought with the clarity of order. The other, with the chaos of pain. They circled through ruin. They danced the last dance.

Steel found flesh. Loki struck—a twisting thrust—and Heimdall staggered, blood darkening the gold at his side. But he did not fall. He did not yield. With a final cry, Heimdall's sword pierced Loki's heart.

The Trickster laughed—a ragged, broken sound—and drove his own blade deeper.

They fell locked together. Two halves of an ending foretold. Fated. Fulfilled.

The wind moved once more, whispering across the shattered bridge.

And the world drew breath... for the last time.

ᛏ

Surtr stood alone. The sword in his hand blazed like the heart of a dying star—not fire of warmth, but fire of undoing. Ash drifted from his shoulders like snow from a burning mountain.

Around him, the battlefield had fallen still. Giants lay broken. Gods slain. Mortals silenced. All paths now led only to flame.

He raised the sword high, and brought it down. The blade cleaved the world. Fire leapt from the wound, roaring outward with a hunger older than stone.

It surged through Vígríðr first, reducing the field of war to molten ruin. The corpses of gods and beasts alike turned to ash before they could fall.

Then it reached further. Across the branches of Yggdrasil, the flames raced, and the great tree groaned.

In Midgard, towns cracked, forests vanished in a breath, and the seas boiled away, leaving salt scars on the earth. Even those who hid in caves felt the fire steal the air from their lungs.

In Asgard, golden halls blackened and collapsed, their proud spires falling like dry leaves. The last echoes of divine laughter and song turned to silence.

In Vanaheim, rivers hissed into steam. Fields Freyr once walked became dust. Flowers curled into cinders. Peace died with them.

In Jötunheim, glaciers melted into floods that evaporated mid-fall. Ice-giants howled as mountains crumbled, then turned to smoke before they struck the ground.

Niflheim froze no longer. The cold was devoured. Even death's breath could not outlast the flame.

In Helheim, Hel stood unmoving as her dead screamed and scattered like leaves in a storm. The long-kept sorrows of the forgotten were erased in an instant.

In Alfheim, light dimmed and shattered. The elves vanished—glowing embers caught in a firestorm.

In Svartalfheim, the forges exploded inward. Molten metal fused with bone. The works of a thousand years oozed into the mountain's cracks and were lost.

And in Muspelheim, the fire still raged—unrelenting, eternal, as it had been since the dawn.

The Nine Worlds curled inward like a dying tree. Their branches cracked. Their roots withered. And above all… the sky split open into endless void.

A silence came—vast, total, final.

Then, at last… the fire dimmed. And what remained was not ruin, but waiting. A breath held in the dark.

The end… before a beginning.

# Chapter 11
# The Seed Beneath the Ash

But not all was ash. Beneath the hollowed roots of the ancient grove—blackened by flame, yet unyielding—two figures stirred. Líf and Lífthrasir, the last breath of humankind, had endured the long night hidden in the marrow of Yggdrasil's memory.

They rose slowly, blinking in the soft light of dawn, the air cold against their skin. Around them stretched a world burned clean— trees reduced to charred pillars, rivers clogged with soot, skies heavy with smoke that no longer choked. Only silence greeted them: heavy, reverent, watching.

Yet amid the stillness, life whispered. From the grove's scorched heart, divine figures emerged, like dawn through smoke. Baldur stepped forward, his presence gentle as spring rain. Light gathered around him—not the blinding brilliance of war, but the first warmth after winter.

Beside him stood Víðarr, the blood of Fenrir still dried on his hands, his gaze turned outward—not in mourning, but in readiness. Together, they watched the horizon.

Above them, the sun rose—not the weary flame of the old world, but her daughter, young, golden, and unspoiled. Her rays touched the land like a blessing, spilling across ruin to reveal possibility.

The gods of old had fallen. Their halls lay in ruin. Their songs had faded into echoes. But memory endured. And in memory lived story. And in story, hope.

Líf and Lífthrasir stepped forward, hands clasped, hearts trembling—but resolute. They would sow what remained. They would walk the bones of the old world, planting songs where ash once fell.

So, the world did not end in silence—but in song. A hymn of healing, of fire transformed to light. Of ash feeding root and seed. Of gods and mortals, entwined once more. Beginning again. A beginning not of glory, but of light born from loss.

## <u>*Of Seeds and the Sun Reborn*</u>

*The ash will settle, the fire will fade,*

*And deep in the soil, the seed is laid.*

*From ruin and root, new life will rise,*

*With sun reborn in younger skies.*

*The gods are gone, but not their grace,*

*Their names still whispered in time and place.*

*So speak their tales by hearth and flame,*

*And shape the world in their mighty name.*